A MIRROR FOR WITCHES

A MIRROR FOR WITCHES

in which is reflected the Life, Machinations, and Death of Famous DOLL BILBY, who, with a more than *feminine perversity*, preferred a Demon to a Mortal Lover. Here is also told how and why a Righteous and Most Awfull JUDGEMENT befell her, destroying both Corporeal Body and Immortal Soul.

By
ESTHER FORBES

With woodcuts by
ROBERT GIBBINGS

ACADEMY

CHICAGO

Published in 1985 and reprinted in 2006 by
Academy Chicago Publishers
363 West Erie Street
Chicago, Illinois 60610

Library of Congress Cataloging-in-Publication data
Forbes, Esther.
    A mirror for witches.

    I. Title.
PS3511.OM53495   1985   813'.52   85-18535
ISBN-10: 0-89733-154-0
ISBN-13: 978-0-89733-154-8

A MIRROR FOR WITCHES

A MIRROR FOR WITCHES

CHAPTER I

1

*Certain Examples to Show Doll Bilby not alone among Wo-
men in her preference for Evil. The Cases of Ry, Goose, Leda,
Danaë, etc., cited.*

IT has long been known that, on occasions, devils
in the shape of humanity or in their own shapes
(that is, with horns, hoofs, and tails) may fancy
mortal women. By dark arts, sly promises of
power, flattery, etc., they may prevail even upon
Christian women, always to the destruction of
these women's souls and often to that of their
bodies.

For in Northumberland, Meslie Ry was burned
in 1616 because she had taken a fiend to love.

A few years later, Christie Goose, a single
woman upwards of forty years, suddenly flew
lunatic — and that upon the Lord's Day. Then
she did confess that each night and every night
the Devil, wickedly assuming the shape of Mr.
Oates, God's minister at Crumplehorn, Oxon.,
came to her through her window. This fact
amazed Crumplehorn, for Goose was of all

women most pious, and had sat for years in humble prayerfulness at the feet of Mr. Oates. Some were astonished that even a devil should find need for this same Goose, who was of hideous aspect.

There was a young jade, servant in an alderman's house in London, who, although she confessed nothing and remained obdurate to the end, was hanged and then burned because she bore a creature with horns on its head and a six-inch tail behind. Such a creature the just magistrates determined no mortal man might beget, although the saucy wench suggested that an alderman might. Moreover, certain children in the neighbourhood testified that they had twice or thrice seen 'a burly big black man' sitting on the ridgepole.

Some assume that as the gods of antiquity were in no way gods (being seekers after evil — not after light), they should therefore be considered caco-demons or devils. The Reverend Pyam Plover, of Boston, has written learnedly on this subject, saying, in part, 'For is it not possible that the Lord God of Israel, being those days but the God of *Israel*, may have permitted certain of his Fallen Angels to stray from the vitals of Hell and disport themselves through Greece and ancient Italy? Here they revealed themselves . . . in many ways to heathen people, who falsely worshipped them as *gods*. If this be true Zeus might better assume his true name of *Satan*, and let us call Apollo but *Apollyon* and recognize in Mars, Hermes, etc., Beelzebub and Belial. Then may the female "divinities" be true descendants of Lilith.' So one may learn from antiquity (consider Leda, Io, Danaë, and others) how great is the ardour felt by devils for mortal women.

As is not yet forgotten, in 1662, near three-score years ago, a woman called Greensmith, living at Hartford in New England, confessed the Devil had carnal knowledge of her. For this she was hanged.

More strangely yet, lived, for brief space of years, famous Doll Bilby, best known as 'Bilby's Doll.' She flourished at Cowan Corners, close by the town of Salem, but an afternoon's journey from my own parish of Sudbury. Of other women devil-ridden, be it Leda or Ry, Greensmith or Danaë, Christie Goose or La Voisin, little can be said, for but little is known. All were witches (if we accept as witches such women as traffic with fiends), but little else is known. Yet of Bilby's famous Doll, in the end all things were known. From old wives' tales, court records, and the diaries of certain men, from the sworn affidavits and depositions of others, from the demonologies of Mr. Cotton Mather, and the cipher journal of Mr. Zacharias Zelley, we may know with a nicety what this woman was and how she lived, from whence she came, how she grew to witch-craft, how she felt, thought, and at the last how she died.

2

Mr. Bilby sails far to seek out TROUBLE, *and, having found Trouble, nurtures it.*

She was born of a wicked witch-woman and begotten by one who was no better, that is, by a warlock. These two devil-worshippers and, they say, two hundred more were burned in one great holocaust at Mont Hoël in Brittany. Black smoke, screams of death, stench of flesh settled down over town and harbour, causing sickness and even vomiting.

On that same day, by evil fortune, a brig manned by Dawlish men stood in the Bouche de Saint-Hoël. These men, seeing that it was fête day, and curious because of the smoke, the screams, and the stench, went to the holocaust. There they saw a wild child, more animal or goblin than human being. This wild child would have followed her mother, who burned in the heart of the fire, if soldiers had not pushed her back. A priest bade the soldiers let her pass to death, for, being of witch-people, she would undoubtedly burn sooner or later. The Englishmen protested, and Mr. Jared Bilby, captain and owner of the brig, caught and held the wild child, who did not struggle against him as she had against the soldiers. Instead she held fast to him, for even the wicked may recognize goodness. The priest showed his yellow fangs at the Dawlish men. He hated and scorned them. 'Take the child and be gone. She was born of a witch-woman and will grow to witchcraft and do much harm — but in England among the heretics. Be gone.'

The child clung to Mr. Bilby and he to her. He took her in his arms, and she lay corpse-pale and glass-eyed like one about to die. This men remembered. When he put her down upon the deck of the brig, he was badly sweated as though his burden had been more than he, a strong young man, might bear. He told his men the child weighed as though a child of stone. Some thought that his heart mistook him, and that he already regretted the acceptance of so dangerous a gift.

Gathering his men about him and having prayed, he gave thanks to Jehovah, Who, although He had never given him a child of his own body, yet had seen fit to send this poor little one to him. Then he bade his men keep their tongues behind their teeth, telling no one from whence was this child (which in the future should be his child), nor the manner of her parents' death, nor the harm which the priest swore she should live to perform. This promise his men kept for years, but in the end, when they were old men, they preferred to serve Gossip and Scandal rather than a kind master, long, long dead.

For days the child lay like death, only occasionally jumping madly from her pallet, screaming 'Le feu! Le feu! Le feu!' then falling back, covering her face with her hands and laughing horribly. The captain coaxed and petted her, urged her to eat, and quieted her with his hands. So by love he restored her to humanity.

Because of her small size he called her 'Doll,'

8

which name she well lived up to, never acquiring the height and weight of other women. No one ever knew her real age. She may have been seven or perhaps six when she first came to England. Being unable to talk English and at first unable to serve herself, she may have seemed younger than she was. Yet, on the other hand, Fear, Grief, and Sickness often make their Hosts appear older than the fact.

Mr. Bilby believed that the shock of her parents' death (for they were burned before her eyes, her mother crying out to her most piteously from the midst of flame) had broken the reins of memory. He thought she had forgotten everything that lay back of her reawakening to life on board his brig, which was called God's Mercy. Also he comforted himself with the belief that if — as might be — she had learned any little tricks of witchery, or if she had ever been taken to Sabbat or Black Mass, or if she had looked upon the Prince of Hell, or even if (being led on by her parents) she had sworn to serve him, she would have forgotten all these things. She was born again and this time of God and to God, whom Mr. Bilby piously swore she should serve — Him and Him alone. The child had been so vehemently frightened she had forgotten all good and needful things, how to dress herself, how to eat with knife and spoon. She had forgotten the language of her birth.

But of evil she remembered everything.

3

He brings the Foundling to his own hearth and to the bosom of his Goodwife. There the goblin-child rewards Kindness and Mercy with Malediction and Evil. She overlooks the Goodwife.

Hannah, wife of Jared Bilby, would not accept her sterility with Christian fortitude. She railed against the wisdom of God, saying, 'Mrs. Such-and-Such is but half so big and fine a woman as I, yet she has three sons. Goody This-and-That, the jade, can find but little favour in the eyes of her Maker, yet, to *her* He sends more children than she can feed; but I, a pious, godly, praying woman, remain barren.' Which, she wickedly averred, showed the injustice of Divinity. However, by curious chance or mischance, soon after Mr. Bilby set out with his men and brig for the coasts of France and Spain, she found herself with child. Some say the Lord tired of her railing, and, to punish her, first raised up her hopes and then sent Doll to blight them for her.

Summer wore away. The nights grew chill. She was four months with child. Then Mr. Bilby, late one evening, came to Dawlish harbour. With him was his goblin-child, now grown pretty and playful. He arrived home in the black of the night and through pelting rain. The child he carried wrapped in his greatcoat to protect her from the cruel storm. He shook the shutter which he knew was by his wife's bedboard.

'Woman, woman, get up and open to me.'

The woman lay for warmth with her servant wench, Susan Croker. The fury of the night shewed forth the grandeur of God. The wind howled above the beating of the rain. Croker cried to her mistress not to open the door on such a night. It could be no living man who knocked, for it is on such vexed and angry nights as these the sea gives up its dead.

Hannah was a fearless woman. She got quickly to the door, unbarred it, and, in a deluge of wind and wet, Mr. Bilby entered with his burden. Her heart mistook her. She cried out, 'Jared, what have you there in that great bundle?' So he took it to the hearth and, as the women knelt, throwing kindling on the fire, he opened the bundle and out popped the goblin-child. She shuddered away from the fire (a thing she aways feared) and clutched her foster father with her little hands, gazing into his face with round black eyes. Every thread of her spikey hair was tumbled up on end. The women cried in horror that this was no child. This was an imp, a monkey, a pug. But Jared Bilby on his knees protected the foundling, both from the fire and the women's angry glances. He soothed her with his body and kind words, 'Ah, the fire would never devour her.' He was here, and he would never leave her. She was his child, etc. He would always love and cherish her — and the like. The child pushed her tously head under his chin and froze into stillness.

Susan Croker told many that, from the beginning, the child bewitched him. Nor did the affection which Bilby gave his Doll ever seem like the love which men feel to their children, but rather the darker and often unholy passion which is evoked by mature, or almost mature women — a passion which witches, when young and comely, have often engendered with ferocious intensity. As long as he lived he was forever stroking her shaggy black hair, looking lovingly into those button-round eyes, and kissing a wide hob-

goblin mouth which many a Christian would fear to kiss. Hannah was a lusty, jealous woman who could not abide such mean rivalry as that of a foundling child. The woman, who had always been a gossiping wife, now, under the baleful influence of Doll, seemed like to become a shrew. She was steely set in her hatred of the child, al-

13

though she fed her, gave her a corner to sleep in, and taught her some small prayers. With her the child seemed dull, indifferent, but with Mr. Bilby she was merry, playful, and loving. So the one thought her a knowing child and the other a zany.

Mr. Bilby would not tell his wife where he had found Doll, but it did trouble him that the woman so cunningly insisted that either she was the child of a witch or the begotten of the Devil. Even Susan Croker, who was kind to the foundling, had horrid suspicions of her. She could not teach Doll the noble, sonorous lines of Our Lord's Prayer, although the imp was quick to learn worthless things, such as 'This Little Pig Goes to Market' or 'A Cat Comes Fiddling Out of the Barn.'

The child, having been in the house a month, there occurred a chance to show what she could do — that is, what evil she could do.

4

Doll covets a ship for a toy and the whole of her Foster Father's love. She nefariously gains her ends and slays a Dangerous Rival.

The midwife promised Hannah a great thumping boy handsome as his mother, strong as his father. He should either wear the bands of the clergy or walk the quarter-deck of the king's navy. Because her husband favoured the nautical life for his unborn son, he made him a rattle in the shape of a ship. In the hull were seven balls which, when the ship was shaken, rattled. Now Doll was forever leaning against his knees and watching him as he carved out this bauble. As one after another of the seven balls were liberated in the heart of the wood, she would laugh and gloat. It was not a toy for her, but for him who should (according to nature) supplant her in her foster father's love. In her evil heart she must have brooded on these things and come to hate this other child that would possess the ship and Bilby's affection. Her hands were always outstretched to the rattle and she cried, 'Give, give, give.'

One day as they were thus — man and child — Hannah came in from the milk-house. The woman was jealous — not only for her own sake, but for the sake of the unborn. 'For,' she thought, 'what shall he, who gives all to a foundling, have left for his own son? Not only has this wicked girl turned him away from me, but she takes the rightful place of his own child.' Then she said:

'It is not well that a woman in my condition should be exposed to contrary and evil influences. Jared, send away your "pretty pet"; give her to the wife of your ship's cook to keep — at least until I am delivered. Many wiser than I, yes, and wiser than you . . .' Her jaw swung loose as though broke. Her teeth stuck out, her eyes bulged, for the goblin-child, through her mat of hair and out of her wild bright eyes, was staring at her. She stared and moved her lips in a whisper, then she skipped across the room, grinning in diabolical glee. Mrs. Hannah felt the curse go through her. The babe in her womb moved in its wretchedness, and was blasted. The woman felt its tiny soul flutter to her lips and escape. She knew that Doll (being of some infernal origin) could see this same soul, and she guessed, from the roving of her eyes, how it clung for a moment to its mother's lips, how it flew to the Bible upon the stand (in which its name would never be recorded), how it poised upon the window-sill, then, unborn and frustrated, it departed to whatever Paradise or Hell God prepares for such half-formed souls. Hannah began to screech and wail, then fell back upon the bed in a swoon.

The body of the unborn child shrivelled within her, and, when a male midwife was called from Dawlish, he said she had been but full of air. She never was again with child. Some said (and Captain Bilby among them) that she never had been — even on the 'bove-related most famous occasion.

But if, as the most informed and thoughtful have said, the blasting of Hannah's infant was indeed a fact, then we have to hand, and early in the life history of Doll Bilby, an actual case of witchcraft. And is it likely such monstrous power (blasting unborn life with a glance or at most a muttered curse) should be given to any one who had not already set her name to the Devil's Book, and compacted herself to Hell?

5

The New Land holds greater promise than the Old. Mr. Bilby, Ux et filia say fare-you-well to England and take up residence close to Salem and not far from Boston, in the Bay Colony. They prosper. The child grows an evil pace.

In those days England offered little peace to men (like Captain Bilby) who would worship

God in their own way, and in accordance with His own holy teachings and the dictates of their own hearts — not according to teachings of bishops or priests. So Mr. Bilby often yearned towards that newer land which lay far west beyond the Atlantic. In time he sold his brig, God's Mercy, and his freehold. The agent of the Bay Colony, in his office at Maiden Lane, London, told him to get to Southampton with his wife, child, and gear. Within the month he should sail.

Mrs. Hannah protested that if the child went she would not. Then he would humour and praise her, so at last she went, although with much bad grace.

In the year 1663 the ship Elizabeth arrived, by the goodness of God, to the colony at Massachusetts Bay, and in her came an hundred souls. There were yeomen, farmers, braziers, wainers, pewterers, etc., indentured servants, apprentices, etc., and certain gentlemen scholars, etc. But in after years the most famous of all these people was Bilby's Doll, and it is she who has made the name of the ship Elizabeth remembered. There was in the hold a cargo of close to an hundred Bibles, and to this beneficent influence many attributed the quick fair passage which the Elizabeth enjoyed. No one thought it possible that the button-eyed foster child of Mr. Bilby could be a weather breeder. In fact no one thought of the child except to wonder at the foolish fondness which her 'father' continually showed her. They thought of the Bibles below and thanked God for their sunny voyage. Rather should they have thought of the witch-child. For good things, such as fine weather, may spring from evil people.

Also on this ship came one Zacharias Zelley, an Oxford man and a widower. He was no longer young, nor was he an old man. In demeanour he was sad and thoughtful. After some shiftings he, too, like the Bilbys, came to settle at Cowan Corners, and there he preached the Word of God. But in time he fell from God, and of him more hereafter.

The new land prospered the Bilbys and they were well content. The plantation which Mr. Bilby was able to buy was not only of admirable size, well-set-up with house, barns, sheds, etc., but it was already reduced to good order and its fertility was proved. Yet for many years, down to this present day, Bilby's lands can produce little if anything except that coarse yellow broom which the vulgar call witches' blood.

The cellar hole of this house still stands upon the skirts of Cowan Corners, and but six miles removed from Salem. In those days there was a good road before this house leading from Salem to Newburyport. Beyond this road were salt meadows and the sea. To the north of the house lay fields of maize, English grass, corn, peel-corn, barley, oats, pumpkins, ending only at the waters of the River Inch (as it was called in those days). To the south were the adjoining lands of Deacon Thumb. But to the west, beyond the rough pastures, and too close for a wholesome peace of mind, was a forest of a size and terror such as no Englishman could conceive of unless he should actually see it. It stretched without break farther than man could imagine, and the trees of it were greater than the masts of an admiral or the piers of a cathedral. Yet was it always a green and gloomy night in this forest, and over all was silence, unbreakable.

Many thought the tawny savages who lived within were veritable devils, and that, some-where within this vastness, Satan himself might be found. To this Mr. Zacharias Zelley, having taken up the ministry at Cowan Corners, would not listen. 'For,' he said, 'we left the Devil behind us in England. Seek God in the heart of this majestic and awful forest — not the Devil. When I was a boy in Shropshire I knew the very niche in the rocks where old women said the Devil lived and had his kitchen. It was there he kept his wife. Every holiday I hid close by the rocks, hoping to see his children. . . . Let us leave him there in the Old England, but in the New keep our eyes pure and open against the coming of the Lord.'

Atheism as the good and learned Glanvill, in his 'Sadducismus Triumphatus,' has proved, is begun in Sadducism and those that dare not bluntly say 'there is no God' (for a fair step and introduction) content themselves to deny there are spirits or witches or devils. Yet how sad to see one of the clergy first agree that the Devil could be left behind in England and soon claim there is no Devil, no witches, no spirits. For without these awful presences, who may be sure of God?

CHAPTER II

There is a small smell of WITCHCRAFT *in and about Boston. A straw doll taken to Meeting throws many into confusion.*

In the fall of 1665 two were hanged in Boston for the bedevilment of an elderly woman, her cousin Germain, and her swine.

In that same year Mr. Saul Peterham, a godly, decent man, refused some small rotten apples to an ancient and malicious hag. For this the old crone muttered at him, making an evil sign by her thumb and her nose, and took herself off in great bad humour. Mr. Peterham, on returning to his house, found that his wife — an estimable church woman — had fallen from a ladder she had put to the loft for the purpose of observing the conduct of her servant wench and the indentured male servant, the exact moment the crone had made her evil sign. The elders of the Church had at the old woman and forced her, weeping and on her knees, to forswear the Devil, his imps, and his ways, and to continue more strictly in the ways of God. It being observed that she could both weep and say the Lord's Prayer, many believed the accusation of witchcraft to be a false one, such as is often launched against disagreeable and impotent old women.

By spring there was yet another suspicion of witchcraft in the Bay Colony, and this at Cowan Corners. In a hut close by the seashore, and in great misery, lived an old pauper called Greene and his wife. He was a tinker, but there were better tinkers than he, and he got little work to do. His wife was a proud woman, born in Kent of high rank, yet, by turn of fortune, she was so reduced as to have become the wife of a tinker. Her craft in herbs got her some money and more ill fame, nor was she content to raise and sell the honest herbs of England, but she must continually associate herself with the heathen tawny savages and thus learn arts — doubtless often evil arts — from them. The Indians venerated her, calling her 'White Mother' and 'Moon-Woman.' She went even into the great forest with more safety than any man. She was loving towards these peoples and had much traffic with them, in spite of the fact the Church elders had warned her twice, saying it is better for a woman to keep her own house than to go abroad through the woods alone and no one knew on what errand.

One Sabbath in the midst of the House of the Lord a poppet contrived of straw and maize, with a leather head and a grinning face on it, fell from below her skirts. None at the moment questioned her boldly as to what purpose she contrived this poppet, yet all thought of those dollies witches make but to destroy again, that their enemies may dwindle with the dwindling dolly.

Later in the week three deacons called upon her and demanded explanation. She was distrait, cried out upon them in anger because of their suspicions, and said she had but made a toy for Bilby's poor little Doll, who, she said, was beaten and cruelly used by that shrew Hannah. The incident was then dismissed except for a public reprimand for a woman so depraved as to put into the hand of a child a toy upon the Lord's Day and in the Lord's House. After this the Greenes lost what friends they had, and no one came commonly to their hut upon the salt marsh but Bilby's wicked Doll.

On a February night Hannah Bilby woke overcome with retching and vomiting. In the morning Mr. Kleaver, the surgeon, being called, took away two ounces of blood from the forearm; still she continued in wretched state three days. By the oppression on her chest and especially because of certain night sweatings and terrors, she became convinced she was bewitched and frankly accused Goodwife Greene. Mr. Zelley roughly bade her hold her tongue (this being but one of many times when he befriended a witch) and declared there was no reason why Greene should wish her harm. At which statement many were amazed, for they thought every one knew that Greene loved little Doll and hated the foster mother because of her cruelty. Through all the clustering villages — Salem, Ipswich, Cowan Corners, etc. — it was whispered how Doll had surrendered to Greene either parings from Mrs. Hannah's nails or hair from her body, and had thus given Greene the wherewithal to work magic.

Within a year all suspicion seemed to have passed away from Goody Greene, but in a hundred ways more doubts gathered about the child and she was whispered of. Mrs. Bilby told many, here one and there two, usually with entreaties for prayers and commands for secrecy, that the girl was born and bred a witch. She told how her own unborn son (that thumping boy) had been blasted. She told them to watch — was not Mr. Bilby himself bewitched by her? So it seemed to many. There were no clothes fine enough in Boston for his dear Doll — he needs must send to England for them. Sometimes he held her on his knee — and she a girl of thirteen or fourteen. Even when the elders and the minister came to call on him, and Hannah, as befitted her gender, withdrew from the room, Bilby would keep his ridiculous hobgoblin squatting at his feet. As he talked, he patted her shaggy, spikey, hair.

The child had nothing to do with children of her own age, nor did godly parents wish their children to play with her. For the most part she was a silent thing, stealing about on feet as quiet as cats' paws. To her foster father she was pretty and frolicsome. To Goodwife Greene she was loving, and stole from the Bilby larder food for the wretched paupers. With her mouth she said little to any one, but her eyes spoke — those round button eyes, and they spoke secret and evil things.

2

Monstrous facts regarding Doll's earliest youth which Mr. Zelley repeated almost twenty years after her death. How she attended Black Sabbath, etc. How she saw the Devil in Brittany and probably swore to serve him, etc.

When the time came late in his life that Mr. Zelley, being old and broken, was accused of witchcraft, he told, after long questionings, much that he knew about Bilby's Doll. For instance, he said she never forgot one of those wicked things which she had learned of her parents in Brittany.

It is true, the shock and horror of their death caused such mental anguish it seemed to her a black curtain (much like the smoke of the holocaust) dropped down upon her life. All that was actual in her life was before the curtain — that is, after her parents' death; yet all that lay behind this curtain did exist for her — only infinitely small and infinitely far away. To see (for she did not call it *remembering*) what lay behind this barrier, she had to think and think only of blackness. Soon was her industry rewarded. Behold, the blackness disintegrated and little by little she saw strange scenes in piercing clarity, yet all in miniature. She saw these visions as though she were above them — say from the height of a church steeple, and she saw her own self, a little shaggy girl, walking below.

If no one disturbed her, if Mrs. Hannah did not cuff her for idleness, she could watch the movements of these people for hours. There were her father and mother, other witches and warlocks, phantom beasts, fiends, imps, goblins, fairies, and always her own self. Sometimes these people and creatures grew so small they were scarcely more than shifting sands. Yet the smaller they grew, the more intense was their actuality. Mr. Zelley said that she observed that when these images, visions, or what you will, were presented to her almost as large as life, they were vapoury and hard to see, but when they were no larger than a grain of sand she could see everything — the little frown on her father's forehead, the scales on the imps' shoulders, her mother's teeth as she smiled, even the nails on the hands of her own self; yet how small must have been those hands when the whole body of an adult was no more than a grain of sand!

Mr. Zelley, an old and broken man, was commanded to tell further. What would she see — on what business would these folk be about?

She would see naked men and women with goats' horns on their heads. They danced back to back. As they danced, they cried 'hu hu hura hu,' in the manner of witch-people. She would see the sacrifice of a black kid, and the crucifixion of the sacred wafer. Did she ever see the Devil himself? Witch-people often select one of themselves to be, as it were, high priest in their infernal synagogue. Him they call devil. Such a one she often saw. He was young and lusty and dressed in green leaves. When they danced their sarabands, no one jumped as high as he. He was a pretty man and women loved him. It was only on Black Sabbath he had such power over men and women. At other times he was a cordwainer.

This devil that she saw was but a mock devil. Did she never see that Scriptural Devil — that Foul Fiend Lucifer? Ah, that she could never quite recall — not even with the powerful help of her strange minute images. It is true that after hours of application she would sometimes see a woman whom she knew to be her mother walking through great oak woods (mistletoe-infested) and with her, clinging to her skirts, was a child. The child was her own self. A great light pierced the green gloom of the forest and where it fell stood a man. He was an aristocrat, carried a small rapier with the hilt of which he toyed; he was dressed in green velvet, had a handsome, ruddy face, and loving blue eyes. Nor had he horns, she said, and if a tail, he kept it to himself; but his shoes she noticed were unsightly, as though contrived to accommodate clubbed foot or cloven hoof.

To him her mother knelt, and the child knelt also. The mother said she had a little servant for him, who she promised would obey him in all things. 'What shall I do with so little a one?' But he caressed her with his hands. His touch was cold as ice. Even to remember that touch raised the gooseflesh upon her. It was searing as the hands of Death. She never saw this particular scene enacted before her without experiencing a physical shock — pleasant and yet repellent. Then she could see the child accept the Book the man offered her, and she always made a mark in the Book with blood drawn from her own arm. But the end of this particular and much-loved vision was always the same and always disappointing, for she saw herself and her mother sitting by the hearth. Her mother was stirring the pot and as she stirred she talked, telling the story of a little girl who had walked with her mother in a great wood, had met the Devil, and had sworn to serve him. So it was Doll Bilby never could be sure whether or not she had actually promised to serve the Foul Fiend and had made her blood-mark in his Book, or whether it was but a tale told by her mother.

At first she felt no terror of the strange phantasies which, waking and sleeping, were always before her eyes, but as she grew to young womanhood, this uncertainty as to her true status came greatly to worry her. If she had indeed signed the Book of Hell, then was she utterly damned, and there was no hope for her. If she had not, then might she, by prayer, watchfulness, etc., escape into Paradise. Thus she endured great anguish of spirit. At last the Soul, which ever turns and struggles in the heart of man, turned uneasily within her and she tried to forget all the evil which she remembered — even the voice of her mother, crying out piteously to her from the midst of flame.

Then Conscience — that gift from God to man — raised *its* head, and she lay and moaned upon her bed, listening to the holy voice of Conscience, asking her over and over, to her utter weariness, what have you done — what have you done? So she applied herself with burning intensity to the ways of religion, and it was then, said Mr. Zelley, he first came to ponder upon her, although she told him nothing of herself or of her past until some years later. But all her pious exercises were performed without that pleasure which the good Christian habitually manifests, but rather with the terror of a lost soul. Mr. Zelley kept a diary, and in that diary he wrote (Doll being at that time in her sixteenth or even possibly in her seventeenth year) a wanton suggestion, 'I mark with interest the religious fructuations of Miss D. B. but fear she fruits without roots, and but let a man, perhaps, Titus Thumb, come into her life by the door, and then shall God but pass out by the window . . .' and more light and blasphemous talk, suggesting slyly that there may be some resemblance between the carnal love of body and the spirit love of soul.

3

A good young man is taken in a witch's net.

This Titus Thumb, to whom Mr. Zelley referred, was the oldest child and only son of

Deacon Ephraim Thumb, whose lands lay south of and adjoining to the lands of Mr. Bilby. There had always been intimacy between the two farms, for the men of one helped the men of the other at harvesting, planting, and building. The two women were gossips. The two men were cronies. Titus had been much away because he was a scholar at the new college in Cambridge. For one year he was home again to help in the opening-up of certain new lands. He was a studious youth who hoped in time to prepare himself for the ministry of God. This, however, never came to pass, for God willed otherwise, and, on completing his studies at Cambridge, he remains there, known to hundreds of young Latinists as 'Tutor Thumb.'

He was a young man of special parts and handsome person. He would be a minister and his father was rich. The wenches of the village flocked to him like moths to flame, ignoring often in the exuberance of the chase (for they were unmannerly and bold to him) proper female conduct. They mocked him among themselves, saying he was his mother's darling or cosset; that he would never seek out a woman for himself. They would torment him, pulling him behind

doors and kissing him, pushing their bodies
against him when he could not escape them, etc.,
etc. For which wanton conduct they were well
served, for he would have none of them, and,
keeping the fifth commandment well in mind,
stayed close to his parents' house.

He had two younger sisters, born at one time,
for they were twins. They were sad and puny
children, and many who saw them wondered
that God had seen fit to cut His cloth so close —
that is, it seemed to many that He had but
enough material (brains, bones, spirits, hair,
vitals, etc.) to make one proper child, yet out of
this little He had made two. In answer to this
questioning of Divine Wisdom, Mr. Zelley said
no one body could have endured as many diseases and ills as the Thumb twins were heir to.
Perhaps it was as well to divide up the maladies
as well as the strength. Labour had a falling
sickness. She would stiffen with a horrid din,
foam and go into convulsions. Nor was Sorrow
of much hardier stock. She was subject to night-
mares and other delusions (which Mr. Kleaver
insisted arose from a cold stomach). Their
mother vexed herself greatly over them, and
where another woman might think it well if the

34

miserable things but made a good end and returned early to that God Who had sent them
thus poorly fortified into the world, she was always calling upon Mr. Kleaver or Goody Greene
to dose them, or Mr. Zelley to pray over them.
They were pretty children with soft brown eyes
and yellow hair, fine and finicky, but their limbs
were miserably thin and their bellies somewhat
swollen.

Mrs. Thumb told them not to play with Bilby's
Doll. She feared the girl because her foster
mother said she was a witch. Like most sickly
children, they were poorly trained in obedience.
They met Bilby's Doll, whenever they could, by
the willow brook which separated the two farms.
Of these meetings, however, they said little or
nothing. The mother often heard them whispering and laughing to each other, and, because she
would hear them talk of Mistress Dolly, she knew
they saw her. As they were too feeble to be
whipped or even shaken, she had little control
over them.

She would have been vexed to know that often
her husband, sitting at the Black Moon Tavern
with Mr. Bilby, planned that in due time this
same girl, whom Mrs. Thumb considered too

dangerous even to cast an eye upon the twins, should marry the handsome Titus. On such occasions Mr. Bilby (although he would clap him on the back, and protest his friendship) always put him off — Doll was but a child, not old enough to marry. She had the immature body of a girl of twelve. Give her time and she would grow. Deacon Thumb would not be put off. Was she not sixteen at the youngest? Had not his own mother married before that?

He was most cupidous. He wanted his son to become heir to the fine estate of Bilby. He did not heed what his wife said of danger. He cared more that his son should have a great property in this world than that his soul should be saved for the next. He was not an evil man, for he was a deacon in the Church. He was a heedless man, and too easily dismissed as gossip the true stories his wife forever whispered in his ear, in regard to this same Doll.

Mrs. Bilby was anxious that the girl should marry and so be out of the house. One day she said, 'What shall we ever do with your Doll? There's not a man in the town that would marry her.' Mr. Bilby said that every unmarried man in the town would be glad to get her. Mrs.

Bilby said, 'You mean they would be glad to get a slice off your meadows.' He said he would box her ears for her. She said Doll would be lucky if she got herself a vagabond, or a widowed man, or an old man of eighty. Mr. Bilby boxed her ears and went down to the tavern. Then he told Deacon Thumb that, although it broke his heart even to think of parting with his treasure, yet was marriage the one and only proper state for woman, and he would put her happiness even before his own. Moreover, his wife still hated the girl, even more than she had the night she first saw her, and although a good woman (and very handsome), yet she was hard. He said he had just boxed her ears and suggested that he was now willing to talk of the marriage settlement. He would do something very handsome by Doll. 'For God knows,' he said, 'she is dear to me.'

4

In spite of the Warnings of his Better Nature a young man looks covetously to Bilby's Doll.

On certain days the men of the two farms combined their labours, then Doll brought to her foster father his midday dinner. To suit his fancy she would bring food for herself also. This food she would eat quickly and without speaking to any one, keeping close to Mr. Bilby. On those harvest days, when the sun was bright on the stubble and heat shimmered in the air, the shade beneath the oaks was grateful. Doll Bilby, in the bright dresses her foster father bought for her, looked as fresh within this shade as one of those little summer flowers that go down before the scythes of harvesters. This Titus noticed, and he knew, although never a word had been spoken to him, that his father wished the match and his mother opposed it.

Also he noticed that the young woman, although so small, was made in a neat and most pleasing manner. She was more dainty, more finicky in her cut than the big English girls. He often thought, as he stretched himself to rest upon the earth, that to the eye of a man of rare discernment such delicacy and small perfection might give more pleasure than more opulent charms, yet he never went so far as to say that he himself was that discerning man. Likewise it pleased him that she was shy before him, for he had been over-courted. When he would stretch his body along the ground close to where she sat, she would gaze unsmilingly at him out of her wild, troubled eyes, and something in that gaze — some necromancy — stirred his blood, so that at nights he felt desire for her, and often dreamed impossible things of her.

During all that year of harvest he had no thought for another one but only of Bilby's wicked Doll. He knew the stories of her — for his mother was forever at his elbow whispering things. He knew of her foreign birth, how she had once blasted an unborn child, how she and Goody Greene had afflicted Mrs. Bilby some years ago, making her vomit pins and fur (for to such proportions had the story of the woman's illness already grown), and he could see for himself how she bewitched her foster father out of his seven senses.

As he gazed upon her sometimes the marrow grew cold in his bones. He thought if he were a wise and Christian man, he would have none of her in spite of his own father's cupidity. In his heart he, like his mother, feared her. He could not understand the power she, without effort, had over him, for the very sight of her coming across the hot fields of noon threw him into a cold, dismal, unnatural sweat. Now was his heart set towards this marriage, but he looked with dread as well as joy to that day which should unite her to him. He believed that whatever her secret might be she should deliver it up to him on her bridal. Half he was persuaded that he would find that she, like Sara in the Book of Tobit, had a demon lover, who would strangle any bridegroom, nor had he an angel or a fish's liver, with which to protect himself.

5

A malignant black Bull leads all astray. Young Thumb fears Doll and suspects the creature is her Familiar.

The Thumbs had a young black bull, which, with other neat cattle and quick stock, they had out from England on the ship Fawnley. This bull was a wanderer, breaking stout fences, and seeking out his own pleasure among his neighbours' corn fields, cabbage plots, and herds.

On the last day of April, Ahab, the bull, loosed himself, and climbing a high hedge of stumps, which looked strong enough to hold any creature but an angel from Heaven, he set forth. Having crossed many pastures and trampled down valuable rye, he came to the banks of the River Inch, where it formed the northern boundary of the Bilby farm. The men were far

away burning brush. Mrs. Bilby was at her churn in the milk-house. Doll, a shiftless wench, was loitering by the river's edge, and there she came across the bull. He was knee-deep among the cowslips. Seeing her, he threatened playfully with his short horns, and set off as fast as he could trot with a bunch of yellow flowers dangling from his blue lips.

She knew the animal to be of great value, and that she must quickly give warning of his liberty lest he escape into the forest, and, being set upon by savages or the *feræ naturæ* of the place, become but meat in the stomachs of those little schooled to appreciate his worth. She ran quickly back to the house, calling that Black Ahab was loose

41

and she had seen him head for the forest. Mrs. Hannah, rushing from the milk-house, caught the girl by the arm, shook her angrily because the cows were up and ready for milking, and she was late to her work. She would not let her run to the upland fields where the men burned brush, nor to the Thumbs' farm so that the creature might be caught. She flung her milking-stool and her pail at her feet, and told her to be about her own business, for if she had done as she should have done — that is, if she had made cheese all the afternoon, instead of loitering about the pastures — she never would have seen Ahab or known that he had escaped. Doll sat upon her stool and bent herself silently to her work.

On his return in the evening, Mr. Bilby was angry to find that no word had been sent to his neighbour in regard to the loss of his creature. Nor did Doll tell him that it was his wife's and not her fault. Partly because she was ashamed that he thought her responsible for the loss, and partly because she was a wild girl who loved to run about, she joined the searching party, made up of the men of the two households.

They searched the pastures and the ploughed lands, the fields, the meadows. There was no place else to search but the forest, for Ahab was utterly gone. They searched the forest until it was black night, following the snappings of twigs, blowings, stampings. Not once did they see the body of the black bull. Doll kept to her foster father's heels. Her dress and hands were torn. Her feet soaked with wet. She often called, and in a lovely voice, 'Ahab . . . Ahab.' As often as she cried, Titus knew her whereabouts, and took himself to her side. For on that black night it was she and not the mischievous bull that he was pursuing. He thought how heavy was the night, how awful in their majesty the woods, and how wild and small the dark goblin-child. So he prayed at the same moment that God might deliver his soul from her soul, and her body unto his.

Weary and disheartened at last, all turned towards home. But Doll had lost Mr. Bilby, who had started back with Deacon Thumb. Titus, amazed and delighted to find her alone, walked by her side. Doll bitterly reproached herself that she had not given warning in time. To comfort her Titus said it was only his and his father's fault because they could not keep the beast in bonds. To his amazement he found that it was

43

not with their loss she was concerned, but only with the fortunes or misfortunes of the wretched bull. He thought, has this woman a familiar, and is it that accursed Ahab? So his marrow froze in his bones.

Thinking that she was indeed no bigger than one of those little goblins that live by the hob and bring good fortune to those who are kind to them, and also how there was much about her shape to please a man of rare discernment, he would have touched her with his hands (witch or no witch) and supported her weariness through the rough dark pasture lands. If she would accept this much from him, it was possible (for the night was May night when all young men for hundreds of years have been allowed special license from their sweethearts) she would permit more and more, so that the day's vexations might end joyously. Many times had he felt a vital spark pass from her to him, and he could not but believe that she was conscious of it as well as he. Doll seemed not to realize his intent. As in the dark he approached his hands to her, she floated from him. Before her home was reached he came to fancy she had no body, or that by some charm (strong as that charm she had worked to bind

44

him to her) she now had made a barrier about herself which he had not the physical strength to break.

He thought of Sara and her loving demon, Asmodeus, and wondered if such a fiend might not now be protecting her. And he wished he had never heard that holy story, for Sara, according to Sacred Writ, had seven husbands and each young man in turn had been strangled upon his marriage bed by the fiend Asmodeus, who loved her.

6

A young Christian witnesses an Awful Metamorphosis and shoots a bullet, but not a silver bullet.

The young man's bodily fatigue was great, and his soul tormented. It grieved him to think that when at last he had gotten Doll Bilby by herself (and that upon a May night) it had profited him nothing. That night he could not sleep, but lay hot and lustful upon his bed. When he believed day about to dawn, he got himself into breeches, jerkin, hose, and shoes, and, having drunk a jorgen of ale, he went again to the search of Ahab.

Because there might be danger in the forest, he

took with him his bastard musket. He came out of the house. It was not yet day. There was some light from the east, but it was a specious and unreal light, and the mists and fog from up over the sea were heavy and blue. He misliked the day.

First he looked about his own cow-pens and then about the cow-pens of his neighbour, for he knew the creature loved the company of his own kind and if alive would be like to return to them. There was neither bull, nor sign of bull. With his musket upon his shoulder, he took a path through Mr. Bilby's meadows and came down to the smooth waters of the River Inch. He thought, 'This Ahab is a greedy drinker. As soon as the sun is up he will get to the river and gorge himself with water.' The fogs lay heaviest over the river, and they lay flat and white like piled counterpanes. Steadily the watery light grew from the east. He thought he would sit upon a boulder under a willow tree. The sun would soon shine out and drink up the fogs and dews of night. He kept his bastard musket on his knees, partly because the strangeness of the twilight vexed him, and partly because he knew that not far from him — no farther than he could shoot with his gun — was a path from out of the woods down which wild animals often came early to drink from the river. It was down this path he hoped to see Ahab, and in the meantime he might get venison for his mother's larder. He sat quietly, and a doe stepped out, followed by twin fawns. But these he would not shoot, for their grace and smallness reminded him of Doll. Everything reminded him of Doll — the birds that sang, the flowers in the grasses, even the mystery and silence of the dawn. Yet these things should not have reminded him of a woman, but of her Maker.

In time he heard a crashing and breaking of twigs, and laughed to himself that he had read the bull's thoughts so well, for nothing that lived in the forest would make such a commotion; only a domestic barnyard animal would carry himself so noisily. Nor was he disappointed, for out of the fogs and through the brush came the young bull, looking vast and large in the unreal light of dawn. He thought to let the creature settle himself to his drinking and then to steal up from behind him and catch his halter. So he sat quietly until he saw with astonishment that what he believed to be an Indian was astride him, and, having rigged reins to the halter, was endeavouring to turn him from the water.

To see a rider on Ahab did not surprise him, for he knew the bull had often carried even his little sisters, the puny Labour and Sorrow. It did astonish and anger him to see a savage in possession of his father's property. So he called out roughly and forbade the man to turn the creature away from him. What next happened he never truly knew, for he was sure that the tawny (which at the instant seemed a large and ferocious brave) jumped from the bull's back and made at him with his tomahawk. Titus knelt upon one knee and fired. In spite of the fogs and bushes that partly confused his sight, he took his aim most accurately against a bit of beadwork above the heart of his enemy. Now he saw this boy or man most clearly, the deerskin fringe to his jerkin, the feathers, the dark, angry face, the tomahawk, the patterns made by beads, and he knew that his aim was accurate and good; yet, even as the bullet sped to its mark, the Indian was there no more, and instead stood Doll Bilby with her hands clasped to her heart.

He knew the bullet went through her. When he first saw her, she was still staggering from the impact, but, when he reached her side and pulled away her hands (crying out and lamenting that he had killed her), there was no mark of blood upon her grey gown, and she assured him in a weak and frightened voice that she was unhurt. This gown Doll had on that day was made of strong fustian, and, as Mrs. Hannah always said, it had not a hole nor tear in it. Yet the next time Doll wore it there was discovered above the heart a minute and perfect patch, put on, evidently, to cover a hole no larger than a sixpence.

So great and so unreasonable was Titus's love for Doll, he at first hardly considered the awful metamorphosis he had witnessed. Instead he was sick to think how close she had been to death.

As this story (which has just been set down in its true form) spread through the village, it grew incredibly larger in the mouths of certain people, and yet in the mouths of others it dwindled down into nothing. For the former of these insisted that Doll did not come alone, but was escorted by a vast troop of infernals, witches, etc., and that Ahab spoke to his master, making sundry infantile observations, such as might occur to the intelligence of a beast. Those who would make nothing of the story (and among these was Mr. Zelley) said Titus was no solid rock upon which to build the truth, and that his fancy had ridden him. There never had been an Indian upon the bull's back, only Doll. He never had seen the beads, fringes, tomahawk. When he shot, his aim was confused and he had gone wide the mark.

Mr. Zelley, in his diary, quotes Scripture in regard to this curious incident, saying in part that Our Lord warns us against the putting of new wine into old bottles, lest the new wine prove too strong and burst the bottles. 'So a torrent of feeling — especially when arising from the passions — is of the greatest danger to a weak container, and young Mr. Thumb is that weak container.'

At that moment, however, Titus had but one thought, and that was that at last the wench was in his arms, for she was so weakened by fear (or perhaps from the actual shock of the bullet) she could hardly stand. He comforted her, stroking her hair, kissing her, and saying over and over that he would have died rather than hurt a hair of her head. Concerning the fact that, but a second before, she had been in other shape and enjoying a different gender, he said nothing, for he thought that she might wish to remain mute concerning the matter, and then he thought: 'It was because of kindness, at least if not towards me, towards the bull, that made this modest young female assume another shape. How could she, as a white girl, have ventured to the forest and found Ahab?' So he said nothing. Now that at last his arms were about her, he felt none of the fire and anguish he had endured the night before; rather, it seemed to him, that he was caressing and comforting one of his own sisters. So he set her sideways on the bull, and took her to her own house.

By the time he had reached his father's farm, he was once more swept by such inordinate and passionate desire he could not believe that earlier in the same morning he had kissed and comforted her, thinking her only a child — not even a witch and much less a woman.

CHAPTER III

Young Thumb dwindles. The witch torments him and her foster father discerns that she is not nor ever can be a Christian woman.

FROM the day on which Ahab was lost and recovered, Titus began a secret courting of Doll. Witch or no witch he would have no other. On the one side of him was his father, winking at him and pointing out the richness of Mr. Bilby's fields, the weight of his cattle, the size of his barns. On the other side of him was his fond mother, whispering and whispering, 'The girl's a witch, she'll come to no good end, she'll hang yet, the girl's a witch . . . witch . . . witch.' Of all these matrimonial plans Mrs. Hannah knew nothing. She saw that Titus was much about the house, but, being very proud of her beauty (which was remarkable in a woman of her years), she believed in her own heart that she was the reason for the young man's constant presence. She could not believe so handsome and sought-after a young man could see anything to desire in the ridiculous hobgoblin-child. Doll Bilby flouted him at every turn, yet was he always after her, hungry as a cat for fish.

Many noticed, even by June and still more by July, that young Mr. Thumb was suffering from some malady that sapped strength from body, color from face, and dulled the eye. He was a listless worker in the fields, leaning upon his scythe, scanning the horizon, sighing, and weakly returning to his work. He ate little and slept less, so that his flesh fell away enormously, and, where four months before had stood a hale young man, now stood a haggard. He would mutter to himself, sit out in night vapours to consider the moon as it shone on the distant roof of Bilby's house.

Thus things went from bad to worse. His mother noticed his condition and guessed its cause. She brooded over the young man, and this made him vexatious and bilious. When his little sisters had met (as they sometimes did, in spite of their mother) 'Mistress Dolly' by the willow brook, he would beg them to tell him everything the young woman said to them. How did they play? Did they build a little house of pebbles? Had they made dolls from stones? They would never tell him, but ran quickly away.

The truth came out later. Doll amused them with stories of salamanders, elves, fairies, etc. They feared their mother would be angry if she knew — for she often had said that all the *good* stories were in the Bible, and if a story could not be found there it was proof that it was not good. So the twins ran away and told nothing of their visits with Doll. They often talked to each other, however, after they were in bed, and went on making up wicked things like those she had told them.

All her life Mrs. Thumb swore she knew her son's distress was from no ordinary cause. If that were true, people asked her, how did she come to give consent to her son's marriage with this same Doll? When she was an ancient lady, living in her son's house at Cambridge, she once said: 'I saw my son like to die, and he swore there was but one cure for him — that is, marriage with this young woman whom our magistrates later judged to be a witch. Therefore I said little to oppose the marriage. Then, too, at that time I placed much confidence in the wisdom of Mr. Zelley. He stood at my right hand, saying, "The girl is innocent. It will be a fine match." Titus would cry out in his sleep for this witch-girl. How could I deny him when I thought it the only way to save his life?'

Hannah raged when she learned that the marriage was arranged (although nothing yet had been said to Doll). Bilby could not fathom her anger, for he thought she would be pleased to get the girl out of the house. He did not know that his wife believed herself the reason for Titus's mopings and pinings. Indeed she had ordered for herself a new red riding-hood from Mr. Silas Gore, of Boston, so that she might have finery with which to fascinate the young man.

At last Doll knew she was to marry the good young man, for her foster father told her so. He told her roughly, for his heart broke to think of losing her to another. Sorrow made his tongue unkind. She would not listen to him, but, laughing, clung about his waist, saying she would never leave him, that he was the only man she could ever love. He wanted to keep her with him forever, but he knew that she was a strange girl, not like others, and he believed that if she were married she would become less secret and, having a house and children of her own, she would be happier.

Then, too, he knew that his wife was cruel

to her, and he thought that it would be better for her to live under a roof where there was only love. It was in vain that he told her that she was now a woman grown, and it was time that she went about the business of women — that is, the bearing and raising of children. Did she have a deep aversion for her handsome and godly young neighbour? Would she not be proud some day to be a minister's wife? No, no, never, never — she only wanted to be his dear foster child. He hardened his heart against her, and unwound her arms from about his waist. He told her to marry young Thumb, or to think up better reasons why she should not. He would not have such an ungrateful, stubborn woman about his house. If she did not wish to do as he wished, she could find another place to live. He never meant such hard words. He acted for her own best good. He pushed her from him, and made off to the fields.

She overtook him in a field of flax where the flowers were even bluer than the rare summer sky. The air was heavy with the murmur of bees. She flung herself on her knees and caught him by the long blue smock he wore.

'Father,' she cried, 'wait, wait, I beg of you.'

56

She put her hands over her face and wept. He could have wept himself to see her thus. He hardened his heart and would have pushed by. She cried out she had something to tell him, so he waited silently, but without looking at her, for he was afraid that at the sight of her his heart would melt. She seized him by the hem of his smock and began to talk in a hoarse voice and a roaring voice like nothing he had ever heard out of her before. She had something to tell him, she said. There were reasons why she could not marry, especially not a young man who wished to be a minister. She feared she was not a Christian woman. She looked up at him from the ground, and he looked down upon her. Their eyes met, and in one horrid instant Mr. Bilby realized what it was she meant, why she feared she might not be a Christian woman. Of Evil she remembered everything, and at that moment he knew it.

He did not dare question her. He did not dare know what she knew. He essayed to comfort her and said he did not care who her parents really were. It mattered no more to him than who might be the sire of the cat that caught the mice in his barn. He also said what was not true, for he assured her that what one may have done or promised at a very tender age had no importance in the eyes of God. So he talked vaguely, and made off to his labours.

She left him and went to a secret spot she had among the birch trees on the hillside. She was not comforted, and her heart was hard set against the thought of marriage.

Those things which Doll told Mr. Bilby frightened him. He went straight to his neighbours that same afternoon and said the time had come when Titus, with his own tongue and in his own body, should do a little courting. Titus said how could he when Doll was never a flea-hop from her foster father's heels? Thus it was arranged. Doll, that very night, should be left alone in her father's house — Bilby and wife should go to Thumb's. Titus would come to her, court her, and persuade her to marriage. After a sufficient time, all would return to Bilby's and celebrate the happy betrothal with sack-posset, hymns, psalms, prayers, etc.

To this Titus and all agreed. Even Doll had nothing to say, but at her foster father's bidding she put on her most wanton dress — a giddy dress of scarlet tiffany such as no pious woman would wish to possess.

2

A woman is seized by a Frenzy. And how a man may court without profit.

Now, when she found herself alone, she ran back and forth, back and forth, through the house. She locked and barred everything. She locked the cupboards and the doors and shuttered the windows. She went to the attic and locked the trunks, the boxes, the cribs, and the cases. She went to the cellar and bolted the door. Doors she could neither bolt nor bar, she barricaded. Even when this was done, she could not stop her strange running round and round the house, sometimes turning in small circles like a dog gone mad. She said over and over to herself, 'I must be a witch, for I can feel myself weaving a charm.' So she ran fast through the house, but here was nothing more to lock.

It was not yet seven o'clock and the evening was still light. Yet so closely had she barred and shuttered everything, the house inside was dark as midnight. Then she got old blankets, and in the end, in her desperation, new blankets, and tried to stuff the gaping chimney hole in the fire-room so that the whole house should be utterly barred and tight. But all the time (as she after-

wards told Mr. Zelley) she would ask herself,
'Why, why do I do these things?' In the midst
of her most desperate work with the chimney
hole, she would stop and begin to run through
the house — unable to stop herself. She thought
to herself that she was working some charm or
rather some charm worked within her. She was
powerless before her great need to run back and
forth, back and forth, through the locked and
barred house.

Titus Thumb, dressed as though for a bridal
and carrying a nosegay of lad's-love and a
turkey-leather psalm book for gifts, came proudly
to the house, knocking to be let in. Doll heard
him, for she was crouched upon the cold hearth
of the fire-room, striving to stuff the chimney
hole. She thought, 'I will let him in, and then
he can do this thing better than I.'

Titus was astonished to find the house dark
and his lady's hair a ragged black mat on her
shoulders, her gay scarlet gown disordered and
torn open at the throat, as though she had but recently wrestled with an enemy. And her face
astonished him, for her cheeks were bright red.
Fuller and more beautiful than ever before, her
eyes glittered indeed like a goblin's and her wide

mouth was pulled up at the corners in a wicked but most provocative smile. She, in the dark house, seemed more like imp or puck than human woman. All that was human in him — that is, intelligence, conscience, reason, and so forth — was afraid and bade him turn back; yet all that was animal in him — that is, the hunger and desire of his body — urged him to enter. So he entered.

Already that awful necessity that had made her run so madly through the house was gone. She explained the blankets by the cold hearth, saying that they were damp, and that she had planned to build a fire and dry them out. So he built a fire. She explained her dishevelled condition. She had heard a rat in the cellar and had taken a poker and hunted for him. Could he not at that moment hear the rat scampering in the cellar? So he took a light and a poker and went to the cellar, and Doll, a little ashamed and frightened, quickly ordered her clothes and hair, and unlocked everything she could before he returned. Yes, he said, he found a rat and he had killed it. This surprised her, for she had really heard no rat, and the thought came to her that perhaps the Devil had sent that rat to excuse her conduct.

The young man sat on the settle with his head in his hands and prayed God to deliver his soul from the woman's soul, and her body unto his. At last he spoke to her, his face turned away from her. He told her that she knew why he was come. He wished to marry her, and that he would be to her a true and loving husband. No, she said, she could not marry him. He was surprised, for Mr. Bilby had told no one of the young woman's aversion to marriage. He had understood that he had only to ask and she would assent. He told her that it was all settled — the very spot on which their house should be built. How could she now so coldly say no? She only said again that she could not marry him — nor any other. 'If that is so,' he said, 'I'll take my hat and go.' But why, if she had no idea of marrying him, had she so kept him at her heels? She had not kept him at her heels. She was always trying to rid herself of him. She knew that was not true. The very way she drew back from him was the surest encouragement a man could have. She said she thought he was talking nonsense. Her eyes glittered at him, round and bright in the firelight, like a cat's.

He was afraid. He got up. He said again that

he would take his hat and go. 'I wish you would,' said Doll. They could not find his hat. It seems that, while Doll was straightening herself and ordering the house (Titus at the moment ratting in the cellar), she had by chance picked up his hat, with many other things, such as the sooty blankets, and had stuck them under her own bed. So now they could not find his hat.

The young fellow was afraid, and now, as never before, he believed she was a witch. His blood pumped through him as though about to burst the veins; he knew that she wished this hat to work further charms upon him. But if she were so set upon charming him, making him her slave, why would she now have none of him? Why should she torture him, making him love her past all human endurance, and yet now so coldly dismiss him?

Doll said she was very sorry about the hat. 'Oh, it is not the hat,' he cried in despair, his head again in his two hands, 'but, my dear Doll, why will you so torture me? Have I ever been anything but kind and respectful to you? Look what you have done. A year ago I was twice the man I now am. You have done it. You've sucked the strength and manhood out of my

63

veins.' Then he talked strangely so that she could not at first understand him. At last she understood him well. He believed that she had cast a witch spell on him, and had thus made him love her so beyond all reason. For, as he frankly told her, she really was not so wonderful nor half so beautiful, etc., as he had come to think her. He said he could remember back three years ago when he thought her a scrawny, rather ugly, little thing with too big a mouth.

All this made her very angry. She jumped up and down in her rage — more like an imp than ever — and screamed at him to be gone. She ran into her own room and came back with his hat — for she had guessed where it really was, but had not found an opportunity to get it for him. She jumped up and clapped the hat onto his head, pulling it down so sharply over his ears that she bent them, and continued to scream, 'Go! Go! Go!' He grabbed her roughly by the arm, called her witch, hellcat, succubus. She turned and bit his wrist, so that it was marked for days. He pulled her off him, shook her with great fury, and flung her from him so that her head struck against the settle and she moaned in pain. Her plight touched his heart infinitely, and he knew that, witch or no witch, she was his dear, his own girl.

So the parents and foster parents, returning, found them. The man, a valiant officer in the militia, a scholar, and the heir to a fine estate, was convulsed with weeping and sobbing. The girl lay terror-stricken in the corner, as harmless as a trapped rabbit. Mr. Bilby had no idea that Titus had flung her into this corner. She was a strange child, and he thought she had picked it out for herself. He pitied the terrible (if somewhat unmanly) grief of the young man, and swore that, in spite of Doll's ridiculous and, he felt, unnatural objections, the marriage must go ahead.

Mrs. Thumb took her son home, and Mr. Bilby took Doll to bed, and he comforted her with that more than female solicitude that a man often shows towards children or women in distress.

Mrs. Hannah was in a rage when she found her fine blankets blackened with dirty soot. Nor would Doll offer an explanation to her foster mother, although afterwards she told Mr. Zelley everything.

3

The voice of Hell is heard in the House of the Lord.

Mrs. Thumb went everywhere whispering: 'Look to my son. Is he not bewitched? Look at my boy — so gentle he would not kick a cat, yet you all know that once he shot at this Doll Bilby, and but a few nights ago he struck her and flung her upon the ground. Then he cried for hours. I took him home. Is it according to God and Nature for a man to love thus? Hating her, loving her, loving her, hating her. Would God the wench were dead, but she is not, and he will marry her.'

Every one thought the girl a witch. She went her own way quietly, working as she always did, a little shiftlessly, her mind on other things.

The harvest was late that year and heavy. One year Nature would starve her stepchildren (for so the colonists felt in the new land) with too little, and the next year break their backs with too much. Mr. Bilby, harassed with many things, did a wrong thing. He went to Mr. Zelley and begged him on the next Sabbath to publish the banns for his foster child and young Thumb, and he led Mr. Zelley to believe that Doll had assented to these plans.

66

It may well be that Doll, in some secret way common to witches (that is, through some imp or familiar used as spy), really did know that upon a certain Sunday the banns were to be read. If she did know, she said nothing of this thing to any one, keeping her own dark counsel, and working her secret spells. On a Friday Mr. Bilby sickened slightly, and upon Saturday he could not touch his proper food, only a cheat-loaf she baked with her own hands for him, and a barley gruel. Mrs. Hannah always believed — and doubtless with reason — that the young woman was at the bottom of this sickening and was endeavouring to keep him from the Meeting-House, for when she heard he was set upon going she begged him not to go, saying he was too ill, etc., and must be ruled by her, etc., and sit at home in idleness.

But he would not be persuaded, and he went to church as always. She rode with him upon the pillion. Mrs. Hannah rode the fat plough horse.

By the windows and doors of the Meeting-House were nailed the grim and grinning heads of wolves, freshly slain. In the stocks before the Meeting-House were two Quaker women, the one in an extremity of despair and cold (for there was some ice upon the ground) and the other brazen, screaming out profanities and laughing in her disgrace. Upon the roof-walk paced back and forth Captain Buzzey, of the train-band troop, beating his drum in great long rolls, summoning all to come and worship.

Inside the Church Mrs. Hannah and Doll sat together on the women's side, and Mr. Bilby, as befitted his station in the community, sat close to the minister. After certain psalms, prayers, etc., Mr. Zelley held forth from the Book of Judith for the space of two hours. There were announcements by the clerk, etc., and then Mr. Zelley again ascended the scaffold. Couched in proper form, he read how Titus, son of Deacon Ephraim Thumb, and Doll, foster child of Jared Bilby, engaged themselves for holy wedlock and desired the pronouncement of these banns.

His voice was drowned by a sharp and most piteous lamentation. At first none knew from where this infernal sound had come. Deacon looked to deacon, wife to wife. Mr. Cuppy, the tithing-man, ran up and down among the wretched small boys. Mr. Zelley stopped in astonishment, looking first up, as if he thought the sound had come from the corn crib in the loft of the Church — or from Heaven — and then down, as though seeking its source from Hell. Doll Bilby was on her feet, her arms outstretched, addressing her foster father. Her voice rose and died out. None there could ever repeat what it was she said. That noon, in the noon-house, between the two services, men and women got together whispering, wondering, and asking each what it was that Bilby's saucy jade had — to her own unending shame and to the great indignity of the sacred service — dared to pipe forth.

Mr. Zelley — the least disturbed of all — saw to it that Bilby and his beloved Doll be got to horse and to home, without waiting for the second service. He was perplexed and harassed by the occurrence, and refused to discuss with his deacons what would be a fitting punishment for the young woman, although most were agreed that it would be the stocks or the pillory. Instead of listening to the discussions in the noon-house, he went out of doors and stood before the evil women in the stocks, exhorting them in the name of Christ Jesus to repent and to be forgiven. Theodate Gookin, a stout child, mocked them and pelted them with small apples. This action of the child enraged Mr. Zelley more than had the foul blasphemies of the Quakers. He roughly ordered Theodate to lay off his own warm overcoat. This he spread kindly upon the back of the most insufferable of the blasphemers. By which act of charity, he stilled her lying tongue, and reproved the levity of the child who would sport about and enjoy himself on the Lord's Day.

4

Evil cursing bears bitter fruit. Mr. Bilby, though struck down, swears to the innocency of his Destroyer and makes a Pious End.

Bilby went stiffly to his horse, his mouth drawn, his face grey. His wife got on the pillion behind him and soon left Doll (on the fat work animal) far behind. When the girl got to the house, she did not seem to understand why her foster mother shook her fist, spat, and made at her with a warming-pan. She did not seem to know that she had cursed the man — that kind man, whom she loved.

Mr. Bilby suffered from a cruel congestion of the lights. Mr. Kleaver said from the first there was little chance to save him. For on one day came the surgeon, with his saddle-bags stuffed with motherwort and goldenrod, and on the next came the minister with his big Bible, and on the third day they were like to send for Goody Goochey, the woman who had the laying-out of the dead — so sick was he.

But he delayed his passage into eternity, fighting death with hardly Christian resignation; for to your true Christian the years spent on this world must seem but as the nine months which the child spends in the womb. His death-day is in fact his birthday into the kingdom of God. Should he fight against death any more than the infant should fight against birth?

There were gathered in his sick-chamber night and day rarely less than ten or twelve people, praying for the departure of this fell disease, or, if this were impossible, they prayed in the hope of giving the shrinking soul a heavenward lift.

Mr. Bilby bade them save their breath, and, although his face was settling into lines of death and he breathed horribly and with an animal roaring, he still begged, as he had from the first, for a sight of his child Doll. The room was then cleared of the pious exhorters, who returned to the Thumb farm and there prayed and drank rumbullion. Only Mr. Kleaver, Mr. Zelley, and the wife remained. Mr. Zelley commanded Hannah to find the child, and Hannah, frowning, went away, but she came back soon and said she was not about. The truth is the woman had struck and cursed the girl so savagely that now, when she heard her name called, she did not dare to come.

The doors of the death-chamber were shut and sealed. Camphor was burned on the hearth; then the wife stood by her husband's side, and, in the presence of Mr. Zelley and the surgeon, asked him three times and in a loud voice whether or not he believed he died of a curse pronounced upon him by his foster child. Mr. Bilby rallied his wits, and, in spite of the agony of his breathing, he stoutly denied the charge. But some (among them Hannah) believe that he was already dead when he seemed to speak, and that an evil spirit had succoured Doll by leaping into the head of the corpse and thus making answer. For he spoke up in a loud, clear voice, and yet one in no way like his own, and the next moment he was not only dead, but looked as though he had been dead for a half-hour or hour at the least.

5

Doll forswears the God of our Deliverance and embraces Beelzebub who prepares (for her instruction) a PROCESSION.

The four days Bilby was dying, Doll spent in the hayloft — night and day. She had overheard the farm servants talking, and she knew of what she was accused and why it was Hannah would not let her into the house. She remembered that strange time when she had run and run through the house, working, she knew, a spell, or rather feeling a spell work through her, and she was sick to think that perhaps she had some power she did not understand, and had really put a charm upon her dear foster father when she had not intended. Perhaps it was also true that unknown to herself she had bewitched Titus Thumb. None went to her or knew where she lay but the youngest of the indentured servants, a good and gentle lad. This boy brought her food and water. When it was night he went to his poor lodgings in the cow-shed and took a blanket from his bed and gave it to her.

From the loft Doll stared down at the house and yard, and could guess, by the close attendance of the surgeon and the clergyman and by the multitudes gathered to pray, how sick he

was. Every morning she saw Hannah go early
to the dunghill and catch a fowl. This bird Doll
knew would be laid for warmth at the sick man's
feet, for under the dark covers the creature lay
quietly and gave off a good and healing warmth,
yet was no bird imprisoned longer than twenty-
four hours lest its heat be translated into the
chill of death.

On the fourth day — that is, the day on which
Mr. Bilby died — Doll determined to leave the
loft and if possible to find Goody Greene, who
would at least tell her how her father did. Perhaps Greene might stay his sickness, for Doll had
more confidence in her and her herbs than in Mr.
Kleaver and his bleeding-cups. At this time of
year the woman often went to the Bilby river
meadows after an herb called 'Love-lies-bleed-
ing,' so Doll, finding the opportunity to slip out
unseen by any, got from the loft and decided
first to hunt for her Sister-in-Evil along the river-
banks. She dared not pass through the town.

She sat by the river until sundown, crying long
and bitterly. She remembered that time Titus
had found her there, and cried afresh — for even
those had been happier days.

Wherever she went she found the flower stems

74

were broke off close to the ground, and she saw
the print of a small Indian moccasin in the mud.
She knew that Goody Greene (being a pauper)
wore these moccasins and that her feet were
small, so she followed this trail, and this led her
to the great forest. Here she paused, for she
feared it. But she feared the cruel suspicions of
her foster mother more, so she took a farewell
look about her at the pastures and fields, and,
finding a small path (still seeing here and there a
moccasin print), she entered boldly.

It would seem, then, that another of those fits
of senseless weaving back and forth overtook her.
She knew the danger of being lost in this great
wood, and she had not for a long time seen a
footprint. Suddenly she began to run through
the woods on those little paths beaten out by
animals, hunters, and Indians. She could not
pause either to consider her direction or to deter-
mine what it was she really sought, for she had
almost forgotten the idea of finding Greene. The
sun had set and the November night was coming down fast. The gloom and overwhelming
silence weighed her down. She began to think
that she smelt smoke or saw the glimmer of a
fire. Wherever she looked she could see light

smouldering in the underbrush. Sometimes she thought there were hundreds of tiny Indian encampments, with teepees but a few inches high, and, because she knew of Goody Greene's fondness for Indians, she tried to come to these miniature encampments. She also knew that she was lost (although this knowledge did not horrify her as it would a reasonable person), and not only did she wish the goodwife's company, but she needed the warmth even of the smallest fire, for the night was frosty cold.

At last, after much running, sniffing, and circling, she came to a small cleared spot, where she always maintained she found a fire burning, and over this fire was a great pall of black smoke. So she gathered more twigs and fagots, and built up the fire — not knowing that she only made a heap of rubbish upon the cold wet ground. At least her 'fire' seemed to warm and comfort her. She lay back upon the moss and fell quickly into deep sleep.

After some time, she waked, startled, for she heard her name called. 'Bilby's Doll!' cried the voice, 'Bilby's Doll!'

'Yes,' she answered, springing up from her unhappy bed. There was no answer to her 'yes.'

Whatever it was, she considered her 'fire' was almost out. 'Who calls?' she cried, and her voice echoed and the awful silence of night mocked at her in solitude.

Then at last, being wide awake, she realized with terror and dismay that the voice that called her was none other than that of her dear foster father. Yet would he never have called her thus, saying 'Bilby's Doll,' but 'Doll' only.

Then she knew that he was dead, and that she would never see him again. It was his lonely spirit, fresh torn from the earthly body, that had stopped this moment on its heavenly flight to cry out to her thus sadly. She flung herself, moaning, upon the ground, unable to shed a tear. Witches, she knew, have no tears, and she realized with horror that her tears had dried up. She began to pray to 'Dear God in Heaven . . .' She heard a rustle in the forest, and then low and malicious laughter. She stopped her prayer. After a moment of writhing and moaning, she prayed again — 'Infinite Master, Lord God of Israel . . . I never meant to hurt him. He was the only person I have ever loved. I never meant to kill him . . .' 'Why, then, did you curse him?' asked a voice, and she again heard malicious laughter. She would have found relief for her remorse in tears, but there were no tears, nor did they ever come to her again.

She felt the presence of a large and probably dangerous animal about, so she flung more wood on her 'fire.' She listened to its padded feet, and told herself it was lynx or wolf, yet in her heart she hoped and feared that it might be at last a messenger from that infernal King to whom she now was convinced her parents had promised her. For, between the moment that she heard a voice call 'Bilby's Doll' and that moment in which she had felt a corporeal presence in the wood, she had become fully convinced that she was a witch with all the powers that belong to such an evil estate.

Slyly she made one last appeal to Jehovah, for she thought that He might even for so evil a one as her own self make His awful majesty manifest. 'O God, who seest all things, who rulest above, O Great God of Israel, give me a sign, give me a sign ...' Then in her impudence she lifted up her impious voice and commanded God, 'Put back the soul of Jared Bilby, for it is not yet gone far and his body is yet warm. Do this and I will serve You. Desert me now, and I wash my hands of You and Your cruel ways!' The rustling and the commotion crept nearer. No angel this thing which approached her on its belly. She stared, expecting to see horned head and grinning demon face. She saw nothing. She cried once more to God. The solitude echoed her voice with laughter. Then she cried to the powers of Hell below and to the Prince of Lies, 'Great King of Hell, if I serve you, you must serve me' (for she knew this was a stipulation in a witch's contract). 'I will do anything, sign any book, if you will but give me back the soul of Jared Bilby.' But this poor soul was now in the keeping of angel hosts. Not Lucifer himself could snatch it from such guardians. As she thought thus, a windy voice cried, 'Too late, too late.' 'Satan, you shall give me a sign,' she cried. And there close to the ground were two great cat's eyes, larger than saucers. They glared at her with a green hellish light that transpierced the darkness and her very soul.

She cried out desperately to those eyes, 'Whoever you are, step forth. I will do anything, sign any book. Tell me now, in Satan's name, is there no way back to life for Jared Bilby? For it was I, I, I, who slew him — with a witch's look. Oh, kind spirit, if you are old, I will be your daughter; if you are young, I will be your bride — stand forth now to me.'

The yellow eyes turned from her as she struggled with her unhallowed thoughts, and the thing was gone. Far away, mile after mile, a voice no bigger than a sparrow's cried sadly to her, and in great agony of spirit, 'Bilby's Doll . . .' She thought to run after the voice, to catch the naked soul in her hands. Of what avail? Gone already a thousand miles. In the littlest voice, no larger than voice of flea or worm, she heard once more her foster father cry to her, 'Bilby's Doll . . .'

She knew that, as there are certain forms and

incantations for the destruction of life, so must there be others for the rekindling of it. What had Our Lord said before the tomb of Lazarus? Could she but remember the words she herself had said in church — perhaps by repeating them backwards she could countermand the curse.

She fell to the ground in an ague, and lay sobbing dryly, exhorting the powers of Hell. Twigs snapped in blackness about her. Feet padded in silence.

The cold of the night, the terror of her soul, the dearth of food, the sorrow of her heart struck her into a stupor from which she could not move. Through this stupor, in steady procession, and with much pomp and circumstance, a long parade of figures, fiends, witches, warlocks, imps, beasts, familiars, satyrs, and even the beautiful chaste Diana herself, moved in fleshly form: a wicked, most fantastic procession. Goblins were there with faces of cats and owls, salamanders but lately crawled from fire. Basilisks were there, serpents, vampires with bats' wings and horrid mouths swollen with blood. The pretty pink bodies of innocent babes were there, who had died unbaptized, and therefore must stand as

81

servants in the halls of Hell, and with them were
pucks and pugs.

After them rolled through the forest a great
orange cloud — like an old and tarnished fire —
no longer heat-giving. At first her eye could
make nothing of it. Then she saw projecting
through the dun vapours were naked legs and
arms, bits of bodies, and drawn and skull-like
heads with tortured eyes. These were they the
French burned at Mont Hoël in Brittany. Although she might not know them, her parents
were among them. A group came slowly after
these, shrouded and shuffling through the woods.
In the midst of these she saw Goody Greene.
This woman, alone of all the passers-by, turned
and looked towards Doll. But her eyes were
blind.

Last of all came Ahab shaking his black head,
a cowslip hanging from his blue lips. She would
sleep and wake, but the procession would still be
passing by, and every so often Ahab would pass
by. The woods were humming-full with an
infinity of unearthly things. There was con-
tinuous lovely singing — or rather a rhythmic
humming that rose and fell and rose again.

6

With daylight the tides of Hell recede. Doll wakes but to a more determined Evil.

At last she awoke to see, not the procession of Hell, but bright day. The humming, however, still continued in her head, rising and falling, but not going away. She was frozen cold to her marrow. Now the loss of her foster father had become a tiny thing infinitely far away and long, long ago. All her previous existence seemed removed from her as if again a barrier had come down upon her, shutting one part of her life from the next. So, although she thought sadly of the kind man's death, it already seemed one with the destruction of her parents — that is, a thing which has happened long back in childhood.

She recalled to herself the story of a girl who had slept in a fairy-wood for a hundred years, and she looked fearfully at her hands, expecting them to be gnarled with a century. But they were as they always had been. Her hair about her shoulders was black. She thought that it was possible (and at that time it even seemed most probable) that, although her body might have retained its youthful form, a great flight of time had passed. She would go back to Cowan Corners to find the dark forest had swallowed it. There would be cellar holes lost in thickets, where Boston, Salem, Cowan Corners, Ipswich, etc., had stood. She felt herself alone upon a whole continent. Her body had grown so light and so unreal, she scarce could stand, nor was she wholly convinced of her own reality until she observed she still could cast a shadow.

Doll Bilby had always longed for the comforts of religion, so it was natural that she, having as she believed just witnessed a manifestation of her 'god,' should now reverently stand and give thanks. She called upon her Father in Hell, thanking him that he had made manifest to her visible proof of his greatness. She called upon her father and mother, blessed them in the great name of Hell, and promised to serve them. She called upon all that vast host of evil things, blessed them, and promised to serve them.

So she floated lightly forth, intent to see the place where Cowan Corners once had stood. Voices called her through the wood, and these she knew were true voices of men, not the eerie cries of ghosts or demons. She answered, 'Here am I.'

Four men came to her, nor was one of them a

minute older than he had seemed last Sabbath at Meeting. Mr. Zelley cried out in pity, for her five days of despair, suffering, and even the astounding pleasures of the night before, had marked the face of Doll Bilby, altering its pretty childish shape.

'My child,' he said, 'you need not have run away. There is no reason to believe Mr. Bilby's death due to anything but nature. Such a congestion of the lights is not uncommon and often results in death. Doll, as he lay dying, we questioned him if he was worked upon by any witchcraft, and he cried in a loud voice, "I die spirit free."'

Doll wept with her hands over her face. None saw that she shed no tears. But she knew that the springs of her tears had dried in the night. Mr. Zelley kissed her gently upon the forehead, and with that kiss he entered into pact with her, for after that he cherished her and became at last her confidant in all things, even in all evil things. And he had once been a minister of God.

Mr. Zelley walked by her side. The three other men looked at her doubtfully, thinking each to himself, 'This young woman is a murderess and a witch.' They soon outdistanced the

minister and the woman, so it was he alone who
took her back to her own home.

He told her that from now on, for a little space
of time, life would be hard for her. She must live
peaceably in the house with Hannah (there was
no other place for her to go). She must, by a
godly, upright, and virtuous life, and by the
goodness of her conversation and dignity of her
demeanour, give the lie (he said) to all those who
would with tedious rustic simplicity believe her
a witch. Both he and Mr. Kleaver knew Mr.
Bilby died by nature and not by art. She was,
moreover, in all things to trust him. He would
clear her name (he said). He had power among
these people (he hoped). She was to be of good
heart, and the Lord God would be with her.
Also he promised to come to her often, praying
with her, and strengthening her.

So he took her to her door. In the yard they
saw the two indentured servants nailing together
a wooden coffin. A group of serious men stood,
watching them, and discussed the mutabilities
of life, etc. Now and again one helped himself
at the barrel of cider that had been rolled out to
accommodate their thirst (for thirst is like to rise
from serious discourse and ponderous thought).

Mr. Zelley took her within the house. The ovens were fired and pots boiled on the hearth. There was the leg of a great ox on a spit over the coals. The little turnspit dog, which ordinarily served at the tavern, had been brought over to serve for the sad yet pleasing occasion. He turned the spit, as he had been trained to do. His eyes were red and rheumy. The hair was burned away from his hind quarters, and they were red and scorched. Doll remembered how often her foster father at the tavern had given scraps of food to this same miserable small dog, and how he called it 'Old Father Time' even when it was a pup, for it had always seemed bent, wizen, and full of many cares. She turned away her head.

The house was full of neighbour women who had come to help prepare the funeral meats. Doll entered. All found reason they must go to the milk-house, the cellar, the barn, the pantry, or to the best room where the corpse lay and the widow sat in black. Doll and Mr. Zelley were left alone except for a squat and horrid form, who stood its own and feared no woman nor man nor witch. This was the form of Goochey, she who had the laying-out of the dead. She had

a face and voice like a man's. Indeed many believed that she was a man who, perhaps having
committed offence in the Old World, had fled,
thus disguised, to the New. She came from the
Welsh borders, and would never touch a corpse
unless she had first set upon her hands ten iron
rings — one to each finger; for she feared that,
without this protection, the spirit of the corpse
might enter her veins and thus havoc her body.

When Doll saw this dwarfish man-woman
standing in the fire-room, fitting iron rings to her
fingers, she shrank from her in horror. Goody
Goochey muttered at her, and Mr. Zelley was
distressed because he believed she was calling the
distrait young woman a witch. However, such
was the hoarseness of Goochey's voice and such
was the coarseness of her nature, he could not
be sure. She might have been calling her another, no more flattering, but surely less dangerous, epithet. Mr. Zelley sincerely hoped so, for
he was far more concerned with the reputation
of Doll than he was with the good or bad language
of Goochey.

CHAPTER IV

1

Two Women sleep in the House of Hate. Doll Bilby, having ruined the fortunes of a Student of Divinity, now turns her powers upon a DIVINE.

As soon as the harvest was in and the grave of Jared Bilby was filled, winter came raging in with unwonted ferocity. It came in foot after foot of dazzling snow, at first snowing only in the night, the sun sparkling out brightly in the day-time. But by the New Year (the snow already standing up to the window-sills and over the fences) the winter grew black. There was no sun, and such storms blew from out the north and northeast as none had ever seen or heard of before. There was no ceasing of wind, snow, and black days. The sea roared continuously, like a thousand lions seeking food from a false god.

The dead could not be buried. The cattle froze. The wolves went to the barnyards killing sheep, pigs, cattle, horses. A woman found a lynx among her ducks. The deer came out of the forest, joining the dairy herds, seeming to ask

89

food of man and shelter in his barns. Such was the cruel winter that settled down on the dead man's house, where lived his widow and adopted child.

These two women lived alone, shut off together from the world in solitude. They lived almost without speaking and in hate. The two farm servants slept in the cow-sheds, and often afterwards said they dreaded even to enter that gloomy house, where the two women sat watching each other, hating and being hated.

As was his duty, Mr. Zelley came often to see them. The snows were so deep he could not travel by horse, so he came on snowshoes with his Bible under his arm. Each woman he saw separately, praying with her and trying to comfort her. What he said to Mrs. Hannah all heard as soon as the roads were broken out and she was out among her gossips, but what he said to Doll no one knew, although in after years much that she said to him was known. Mrs. Bilby said that once he came out of Doll's chamber like a soul spewed out of Hell. He looked roundabout him wildly as if he had seen a most frightful sight or heard most frightful things. Without as much as a word for the woman (who hoped he would pause and elucidate for her certain problems she had found in Leviticus), he seized upon a bottle of rumbullion, swallowed half of that, and made out of the house as though the devils were after him. The truth is on that day Doll had confessed to him that she was a witch.

Up to this time he had always praised the Christian fortitude, the piety, the humbleness, and sobriety of Bilby's Doll. But after that he came to be much agitated at the mere mention of her name, shaking his head, exclaiming, 'Dear me,' or mentioning the fact that we are all miserable sinners. He was about the Bilby house more than ever, seeing Doll always alone and in her own chamber.

When it was said that Doll was a witch, he would reprove the speaker, sadly bidding him keep such light thoughts on serious matters to himself. Of course the Bible proves to us that there were witches in the days of Leviticus and Kings — but to-day . . . now, he was not sure such things exist.

'Then you do not believe that Jonet Greene . . . ?'

'There does not live a more excellent Christian. Fools call her a witch because she begins to lean upon her staff and she has a wandering eye. Many do so and have such.'

'Nor yet in the justice done upon the bodies of certain witches in Boston?'

'I will not judge of Boston. I speak only of Cowan Corners.'

By these beliefs he gained some friends and lost others. If one does not believe in witches, how can one believe in devils, and if not in devils, how then in Hell? — and Hell is, as all know, the fundamental principle on which good conduct and Christian faith are built.

The women in the Bilby house rarely spoke. Each knew her own duty and did it. The indentured servants kept to the barn, so there was no noise but the swish of the women's skirts or brooms, the rattle of cooking ware, the slam of a door. Even the house dog, grown old and deaf, never barked. The cats, five in all, partook of the silence. They slipped from room to room, eyeing the women suspiciously, but without half the suspicion with which Hannah eyed them.

On a cold night, Gideon, a big malty tom, being chill, sought animal warmth. He jumped upon Widow Bilby's bed. She woke gagged with fear. She seized Gideon and, in spite of the clawing that shredded her arms, strangled him.

The next day with an axe she killed every cat in the house. This brutal slaughter of innocent and pretty pets dismayed Doll almost beyond endurance. She had loved and fed every one, and they often slept upon her bed at night. Filled with abomination towards the woman, she thought at least to give her a headache, or in some way work her a small harm. She looked about for nail paring or wisp of hair with which she might fortify a poppet and work magic against the woman. She found to her astonishment that Hannah evidently suspected her, for any combing from her hair was instantly burned, and she never pared her nails except over a dark cloth which she shook out into the fire. While she did these things, she would look slyly at Doll, as if to say she understood her game, and would take every precaution against her. So she had done ever since her husband died, but Doll did not notice this precaution until February.

Much of the time Doll lay in her own room upon her own narrow bed, and prayed to the Prince of Hell that he send some instructor or messenger to her . . . but thus far only Mr. Zelley came to instruct her. She looked forward to the spring with longing, and because of a dream she had three times concerning a young man asleep in a bed of violets (yet the man she knew, even as she gazed at him, was infernal), she came to believe that in spring, when the violets blossom, a messenger would come.

By February, the roads being broken, Widow Bilby was again about, but Doll in her discontent walked solitary. She saw no one except perhaps once in a long time Goody Greene, and once a week Mr. Zelley (whom she filled full of the phantasies of her childhood). She did not go to Church, and this shocked and angered the whole community, although Mr. Zelley himself insisted that she was too weak and sick to take the hard trip on horseback. Of her neighbours, the Thumbs, she saw nothing. Titus (because of the stories which Widow Bilby told his mother, and she, in turn, told him) went in daily terror of his life. He believed Doll had a poppet of him. If his head ached, it was because she pinched or pricked the head of the poppet. Were it his stomach, lights, bowels, that hurt him, he thought she was rubbing poison on the belly and body of this same poppet. When a black sow he

had raised up by hand suddenly jumped into the
air and fell dead, he thought she had in passing
glanced at it.

Of all things, however, Titus most feared
Ahab, the black bull, who had, from the day
Doll found him in the forest, changed his gentle
nature to one most ferocious and perverse. He
urged his father to butcher the animal before it
took human life. The deacon said it would be
gluttonous to put into the stomach such costly
steaks, roasts, etc., and any man who did so de-
served to have his bowels rot.

2

*Showing that the Sun will always shine again, no matter how
black the Winter.*

The winter had come early, but (contrary
to country superstition) it remained late. For
April was full of the racketing of wind, and May
was drenched and all but drowned in rain. Not
until the end of that month did the earth rally
from adversity, and there come still and sunny
days. The skies were of heavenly blueness,
crossed only by herds of fleecy clouds, as sweet
and innocent as wandering lambs. The grass
grew green and was prettily pied with multitudes

of little flowers. The fruit trees glanced but once at sun and sky, then burst into rapturous blooming. The beauty of these trees is not idle and barren. Their deeds (that is, their fructuation) is as good as their promise (or blossoming). Man may enjoy the loveliness of these flowers, knowing that their loveliness is one of accomplishment.

Special lectures were held at the Meeting-House, giving thanks (where thanks were due) for the beneficent weather, the fertility of all things, the abundance of fish, game, wild foods, and good health of the community. In his praying Mr. Zelley (so it was observed) twice asked with particular passion that the old hatreds, the old jealousies, and the old cruel superstitions might be left behind, and that, in the new land, the spirit of man might break forth as a chick breaks the egg.

The widow's house had stood fast-shuttered for six months. Now it was open to sun and gentle breeze. Doll had been pale, sad, all winter; now she felt the gladness of the earth singing about her in the sweetest voice, calling her to set aside the dark mantle of the soul to take on joy, hope, and even pleasure. She felt frolicsome (as she had often felt with her foster father) and played with the calves and colts, secretly met the Thumb twins by the boundary brook, and filled them full of devilish lies.

She went again to the Meeting-House, and even wantonly enjoyed herself during service, for she found that (such were her latent powers for harm), by merely twisting her fingers together and staring hard at Deacon Pentwhistle as he led the psalm singing, she could twist his throat so that he broke off into a coughing fit. Once, on seeing Titus enter the pasture where Ahab grazed, she slyly and only by thought ordered the creature to have at the young man. Behold! She had the inimitable pleasure of seeing Ahab make at him, and Titus barely reached a tree in time to save his limbs. If Ahab had gained too much on this swift and willing runner, she would have crossed her legs and this would have stopped the bull, for she wanted her old lover frightened, but neither maimed nor slain.

Mr. Zelley continued to wrestle with her in prayer, begging her to believe that she could not be a witch because he (being little better than an atheist) thought such things could not exist. He always claimed that he strove to save her soul.

97

She rewarded him by destroying his. She went often to his house and read in his library, especially of all such books as the 'Malleus Maleficarum' and 'Sadducismus Triumphatus,' etc., which treat of witches and witchcraft, for she was unskilled and wished to learn proper charms and methods for working evil. She also questioned Goodwife Greene. Still she never could learn (except by accident) how to do any of the things she wished. She could not even summon the Devil, who, when he came, came as pleased him — not to her order.

3

An Intimation comes to Doll that some Infernal is about. She believes that he whom she (in wicked abomination) worships will soon send sign to her.

On a morning she awoke, knowing she must go to Greene's house. 'I must see Goody Greene,' she thought. 'I must talk to Goody Greene.' She left the pots unwashed, the room unswept. She put on neither coat nor hat, but went as she was, for the day was warm. Now the new year seemed to promise great things, and she felt confident these things she would find. There every happiness close to her, hiding, waiting to be found. Through these pleasant and cheerful thoughts came racketing the clangour of a brass bell and the terrible blasting of a fish horn, and the voice of man (in this case the voice of the town crier) tolled out to her and to all the world those things that were lost.

Mr. Minchon, the crier, put the fish horn under his arm and took the brass bell by the clapper.

'Gone away!' he cried. 'Gone away! Gone away! Four pirates from the Boston Jail, one day before their trial. Calico Jack and Black Pig Murch, Ben Bottle and the Bloody Shad. Likewise, from the pasture of Deacon Thumb, one priceless bull known to you all, the young bull Ahab.' (Ding-dong! Ding-dong!)

'Lost or stole, lost or stole, a wallet and the money in it of Captain Tom Buzzey, for he put it on the tavern step, turned, and it was gone. Lost or stole, the wallet of Tom Buzzey — a wallet with the money in it.' (Ding-dong!) Mr. Minchon, blowing again upon his fish horn, took himself and his sad news of things lost or things stolen to the next street corner; there, having gathered a crowd about him, he proclaimed again. He moved again and yet again.

Knowing the matter of which he spoke, Doll could even at a long way recognize the names of the four pirates, for he always began with full lungs, so she heard four times the crying out of these names, Calico Jack and Black Pig Murch, Ben Bottle and the Bloody Shad, but of Captain Buzzey's loss she heard but once, for Mr. Minchon arrived at it with spent ardour and small voice. Doll continued on her way to Greene's hut.

Between the house of Mr. Zelley and the House of God, she met seven Indians who walked the one after the other, with feet silent as panther paws. They were dressed in the paint and regalia affected by their chief men, in the hope of giving to their persons, by external and childish methods, that true dignity which never can come from without but arises only from the soul. The Indians passed (as they always do) without so much as glancing at the white woman, but she gazed hard upon them, thinking that perhaps they really were devils — as many ignorant people then believed — and that the sign or messenger which she had come to look for constantly would be from them. As she watched, a feather floated or rather seemed to be lifted from the headgear of one of these, and, after wavering a second, it came to rest at her feet. This was a scarlet feather with a yellow tip to it. She stooped to it, and hid it in her bosom, looking longingly after the seven chief men, thinking that having vouchsafed her this favour they might sign her to follow them. They did not.

She went her way, but she went exulting, with red cheeks and smiling mouth. The young men she passed at the tavern drew back that she might not cast a roving eye upon them and desire them, for they all knew of the bewitchment by which she had afflicted Thumb. They guessed, by the unaccustomed red of her cheek and the sparkle of her eye, that (spring having come again) she was wandering about looking for a new young man to devour. The young men stood back; Doll went her way.

She came to the waste marshes by the sea on which sat the tinker's hut. She rapped on the door and cried out her own name. The woman did not call 'Come in,' as was usual, and Doll heard rustlings, whisperings, tramplings, within. She thought how this woman, like herself, was a witch. Her heart beat quicker with the (to her) delightful thought that perhaps at that very

101

moment she had discovered Greene in confab with some fiend spirit or familiar, and that was why the door was not opened to her, that was why there were rustlings from within. Then Goody Greene opened the door and with her usual affection drew the girl into her miserable house, kissed her, and put out the stool, a joint-stool, for her to sit on. Greene went on with her own business which was concerned with sorting out into heaps dried toadstools and mushrooms.

Doll stared at her and saw how hard the pulse throbbed in the old woman's neck, how her hands shook at her work, how again and again she swallowed as if choked by an oppressive secret. But the girl could not tell the woman she thought her a witch and say, 'I would like to see the familiar I know must be close by,' for the moment she stopped upon the threshold she was aware that she and the goodwife were not alone. She could feel the air tremble about her; she could almost hear it, all but see it. It was there, close in the one room of the hut, with them. It had not flown at her coming; it had hid itself. She saw that the hangings upon the bed were drawn. 'It is yonder,' she thought; 'the fiend hides in the bed behind drawn curtains.' She was sick with fear, but her hopes rode high. She took from her bosom the feather the Indian had dropped. What did Goody Greene think of the feather? Greene said it was a bright and pretty feather, and proved the Indians to be more skillful than we in dyeing. But did it mean nothing more to her than that? No, nothing more. She put it back into her bosom. What would Goody do with so many fungi? She would mix them with snake fat and cure rheumatics. She said she did not know snakes had any fat. Greene said that any distillation from flesh was called 'fat.' Then they sat for a long time without speaking.

Doll helped with the sorting.

Doll thought to herself, 'Be my friend, Goody Greene; confess you are a witch, show me your familiar, and we will work magic together, for I cannot bear to be so lonely.' The woman set a pot on the fire to make a gruel for dinner. She put three handfuls of maize into the pot. Doll asked her, 'Does the goodman come back for dinner?' 'No,' said Greene, 'I put in the extra handful by mistake.' This was very strange, thought Doll, but in her mind made note of the fact that a familiar will condescend to eat maize gruel like a poor man. It distressed Doll that the woman would not trust her and produce her familiar.

The woman squatted before the pot, Doll knelt beside her, and, because she was sick with bitter loneliness, she pressed her face against the woman's sleeve and said, 'You are the only mother I have ever had since I was a tiny child, and I, Goody Greene, I am the only child you ever had.' The woman let the wooden spoon slip from her fingers so that it was lost in the gruel, and Doll, who jumped up to fetch her another one, saw from the corner of her eye that she glanced at the bed. 'Ah,' thought Doll, 'perhaps she has made herself a popinjay from broom or rags or scarecrow, and calls this thing "son." Perhaps that is what she has about her in this room — and in the bed most likely.'

As they ate their dinner (of which there was far too much for the two women), Doll asked Greene to tell her again some of those old stories by which she had enchanted her as a child. Greene told her of the unfortunate earl's daughter, who consented to a boat ride with a handsome stranger-man. (The masts were of gold, but did not bend before the wind. The sails were of taffety, and did not fill with the breeze.) They sailed three leagues and then she spied his cloven hoof and wept most bitterly, knowing it was no man but a devil with whom she must cope.

Greene told her other ungodly stories from an ungodly antiquity. Doll questioned her at every turn. She must know how each magic trick was worked; she must hear how it was Fair Jennifer of Bageley Wood called her demon to her. Greene told her the true story of how a lycanthropic man, believing himself to be a wolf, killed fifteen in the Midlands before the soldiers got him. She told her of Queen Mab and her tiny tinsel court. At last Doll got to her feet to go. She heard the bed creak, and saw a moving lump bulge out the drawn curtains. But the familiar did not make itself manifest. As Greene stared at the hearth, Doll slyly drew the red and yellow feather from her bosom and, brushing by the bed, she slipped the feather within. Calling a hasty good-bye, she left abruptly, and began to run, for she (in spite of hopes) half feared a great, scaly, black fiend would leap from the bed and on the instant shoulder her, and march off down to Hell.

4

Doll finds an Imp in a cellar. It proves unfriendly to her.

On the next day Doll returned to the marsh hut. Again she found Goody Greene seemingly alone, yet the one room was mysteriously filled with a Presence. That day Greene was making teas, infusions, etc. She had four pots on the coals, and was much confined, in her thoughts and in her words, by watching them.

Beside the hut was a cold-cellar dug into the ground, and in this Greene stored her herbs, her drugs, fats, oils, bottles, pans — all the matter for her trade. She wanted organy, dittany, and galingale root. Doll ran quickly to the cellar. She knew where these things were laid.

She opened the door, which was in the shape of a bulkhead, and ran down the short flight of stairs. Here she had played in childhood, and the strong odours of herbs, roots, and meat oils were fragrant to her. So she paused a moment, sniffing about. There was a rattle on a dark shelf behind a clay crock, and a snake skin shook. She thought she had left the familiar behind her in the good woman's bed, yet she cried out in her horror, calling by mistake to the *true* God — not to the Satan she had sworn to serve; for there, peeking about the clay crock, was a ball of tawny fur and from out the fur glared a little man's face. His features were like an Ethiop's, and his head no bigger than an orange. She noticed, even in the brief moment she paused to look at him, that hands and even nails were perfect. Behind dangled a long ringed tail — a pretty tail of black and dun.

This imp was much offended by her, for it scolded her in strange languages, and its eyes were red with hate. So in terror she, who thought herself brave enough to stand up before Lucifer, fled from the littlest of his servants. This servant she saw again, and the next time without fear.

She ran to Goody Greene, crying she had seen a terrible thing.

'Hush,' said Greene; 'you saw a skull or two, or a snake skin . . .'

'No, no, no, it was alive. It was a little imp.'

'You dreamed it — or it may have been a cat. Cats get into my cellar for the sake of the fats.'

'It was not a cat.'

But Greene knew it was not an imp.

At the end Doll was cast down because Greene

trusted her so little she would not confess the truth, even when she had seen the actual fact of the imp's body, had heard it chatter. She was distressed, picked up her bonnet and put it on her head. There was much work to do, she said. Mrs. Hannah was plucking geese, and she must be back in time to rub ointment on them where they bled.

'Doll,' said Greene, 'I heard you cry out to God for help when you saw the cat in the cellar.'

'I forgot myself,' murmured Doll, and was ashamed that in her extremity she had called upon God and not upon the Foul Fiend she had sworn to worship. She guessed this was the reason both for the imp's rage and Greene's mistrust. 'I will not forget again,' she said.

Goody Greene assumed an attitude which seemed indeed to the girl one of mock piety. She rolled her eyes and said, 'Always give thanks where thanks are due.'

Doll thought she was reproving her. 'I will next time,' she promised.

Then she went away.

CHAPTER V

1

The night crackles with Fire. Hell laughs and a Witch meets
that which she long has sought.

STILL in the month of May, catastrophe came
to Cowan Corners. On three nights, consecu-
tively, great fires broke out. The first took the
noon-house of the Church. The second the rope-
walk of Deacon Pentwhistle. The third took the
barns, sheds, outhouses of Deacon Ephraim
Thumb. This last fire was upon the thirty-first
day of May and the morrow would be June.

The farm servants of Widow Bilby came up
from the cow-sheds. They called to the window
in the attic where Hannah slept (for since the
nights were warm she preferred the desolation of
an attic to the proximity of her detested com-
panion), 'Widow Bilby, Widow Bilby, there's a
great fire at our neighbour's. Shall we not go to
help?' The widow told them to go and do their
best, and God go with them. She, too, would
follow soon. She got into her clothes, and Doll
heard her stamping down the stairs and out of
the house. Doll looked from her window and the

sky was orange. She clutched her throat, for fire terrified her (because of her parents' death), yet it fascinated her (because of her unnatural yearning for Hell).

Will she, nill she, the young woman dressed and, much perturbed, she reached the outskirts of the onlookers. With them she could not mingle, for they feared her, and she dreaded this same fear. She withdrew to a big straw stack, and beneath its overhanging top (for the cattle had rubbed against it) she found herself a hiding-place.

Every able man in the village was there, and half of the women. She saw Titus passing buckets and getting out gear, nor could she have looked at him without some slight regret, for he was a goodly, comely man and a young witch has an amorous eye. She heard the shouting, the running about, the snap and rustle of the flames. Sometimes other idle watchers came close to where she hid, and from their talk she learned that these three fires had all been started by a cat breathing fire. Widow Bilby had said that this same cat could be no other than her old tom, Gideon, now dead a three-month, thus maliciously returned from Hell. Doll heard her own name spoken and saw heads shaken. She also heard that Ahab was still within the vehemently burning barn. Because of his ferocity as well as because of his wanderings, he had lately been closely penned. So far no one had been able to loose him, although several had essayed to do so. The horses, savage with fear, had been moved far from the fire lest they, with the fondness of their kind, return to their accustomed stalls and perish. The cattle were running about the barn-yard, where they interfered with the work, up-setting buckets, etc. Such swine as the Thumbs possessed burned to their deaths, their stench polluting the air. Doll sickened at the smell, for she never could forget the holocaust of Mont Hoël. Until the fire burst the ridgepole, the doves flew constantly from their cotes under the eaves. Some were so singed they fell to the muck of the yard and, trampled under foot, perished.

Just before the fall of the barn floor, Ahab was loosed. With sparks upon his coat, his eyes rolling most horribly, he came out of danger at a gallop. Seeing the crowd, he charged furiously, passing over the bodies of three, yet not staying to gore them, so intent was he on the men who ran. Wherever he went, the crowd melted and the shouting rose. Many believed it was this wicked bull, and not the Hell cat, that had set these fires, for now he seemed intent on guarding the fire and would let no one near it. Doll thought the creature was her friend — perhaps sometime he would become her familiar; but when she saw him coming for her on a brisk and determined trot she ran up the short ladder leaning against the straw stack, not relying unduly on either charms or friendship.

The same moment the roof fell and sparks flew up, rising into the night air an hundred feet and more, until the sky seemed filled with departing souls flying up and up to the Throne of God.

Doll, panting from her vexatious exercise upon the ladder and sweating from her recent fear, found herself upon the top of the straw stack. She was sprawled upon hands and knees. In the fury of the orange light (which with the fall of the roof suddenly was most horrible) she gazed about her. Then she saw she was not alone, for with her was a luggard fiend who stretched his length upon the straw. His eyes were red as though filled with blood. He wore (she said) a costume like a seaman's, except that, where a seaman's clothes are coarse, his were fine and dainty. For instance, the hoops in his ears were not of brass but jewels. She said he had a silk kerchief tied about his head. Upon his breast he bare — as if in mockery of that virgin whose worship the Catholics prefer to the worship of God — the very imp, the little servant, whom she had seen in Greene's cold-cellar. She guessed he was her god, or a messenger from her god, so, crying out, 'Master, master, you have come for me,' she further prostrated herself before him. Now she was no more alone, for this fiend had come for her.

113

At first the demon made no response; then, after a little and with a few high but kindly words, he permitted her to approach. She said she could scarce believe that, after such long waiting and such unanswered prayers, he had at last come. 'Oh, I have been lonely, lonely; I have had no one,' and she sobbed (no tears came).

'Why do you sob, Bilby's Doll?'

'Because I am happy at last.'

He reproved her gently because she had ever doubted his advent, which he said he had announced to her by the lighting of these three great fires. It was his will that turned her steps to the ladder and, as she became too intent upon the fire to notice the summons of his will, he loosed a fierce black bull who urged her up the humble ladder and into his presence.

'And you really are from . . .'

'From Hell,' he said, and showed her his teeth that were white and strong as an animal's. She shrank a little from him. He told her not to fear to approach and touch him, for he was in human guise. There was no sulphur on his person, no blasting fire in his hands. To prove his wholesome humanity he touched her wrist, and she experienced a shock of joy such as she had formerly experienced when her mother had led her to Satan in the heart of the oak wood. This joy she accounted a religious joy — such (so she explained to Mr. Zelley) as a Christian would experience at receiving the visitations of an angel.

Now was she no longer alone in this sad world, for her god (that is, Satan) had come to succour her, or had at least sent her a messenger. She asked him which he was, Satan or lesser demon. At the mention of Satan's name, he bowed his head reverently. He admitted that he was but one of many fallen angels who had left Paradise with the Awful Prince. At first she was cast down, for she had hoped to hear that it was the Prince himself. But she looked again, and marked how handsome a man he was and of what a fine ruddy complexion. She saw how strong were his shoulders, and how arched and strong his chest. She was thankful then that Satan had not seen fit to send her merely some ancient hag or talking cat, ram, or little green bird, but this stalwart demon. She thought, 'He can protect me even from the hate of Mrs. Hannah.' She thought, in her utter and damnable folly, 'He can protect me from the Wrath of God.'

The whole barn fell into the cellar hole. As she

115

looked towards this glowing pit, she thought of that vaster and crueller bonfire in which her soul would burn forever. She thought well to ask him a little concerning those pains which she later must suffer. He laughed at her. There would be, he said, no pain. Those who served Satan faithfully in this world were never burned in Hell. Was not Satan King of Hell? Why should he burn those who loved and obeyed him? She was stuffed full of lunatic theology. The only souls that suffered in Hell were such of God's subjects as had angered Him and yet had made no pact of service with Satan. These the devils burned — even as God ordered. It gave them a thing to do. He pointed out there were no angels in Hell watching out that God's orders be fulfilled, so naturally the devils did not carry out the cruel sentences God meted out to true subjects of Satan. Again he said, 'Why should they?'

She asked him of news concerning her father and mother — good witches whom the French had burned in Brittany. These he assured her roamed happily and at free will, finding cooling breezes even in Hell. When it pleased them, they sat and conversed with antiquity or with the greatest kings, princes, etc., who had ever lived

116

in this world. But her mother was a kindly woman and got more pleasure out of good deeds than from idle conversation. Therefore Satan permitted her to go about among those who burn and give them water or fan away the smoke. Doll was convinced that the messenger had indeed seen her mother, whom she always remembered as a gentle and loving woman.

Was this kind mother aware of her daughter's sufferings? Was it she who had thought to send him to comfort her? No, no. A mortal who is dead cannot see back into life. It was Satan himself who had pitied her and ordered him to her side. Him he bade her worship, 'Truth in and humbly.' At first she could not understand this reversal of many sacred phrases. Later she came to know this blasphemous jargon well. For every night she said Our Lord's most holy prayer backwards — thereby addressing herself to Satan; but what came to her as punishment for this wicked practice we shall see.

He had about him a bottle of grog, and from this he baptized her, 'Ghost holy and son, Father of name the in.' Now he said she was no longer Bilby's Doll. Now she was the Devil's Doll. And he kissed her reverently upon the forehead.

His pretty imp peeked out from within his blue blouse where he kept it. He bade her stroke it. This she did. She said it was a warm and gentle imp, with tired and thoughtful (but not malicious, as she had at first thought) eyes. It was well furred and, if it were not for its wise, sad face and minute black hands, she might have thought it indeed but an animal. She came to love this imp, playing with it and petting it. Its name, he said, was Bloody Shad. 'Why,' she said, 'that is the name of one of the pirates that escaped.' The fiend said he knew that fine fellow well. He had taken his nickname from the imp the young woman now held in her pretty little hands.

The fire was laid and the dawn gave more light than the embers. Birds shook the thin, watery air with their calling. A few men still stood about the fire. The one called to the other that Ahab was in a village garden devouring new-set cabbage plants and terrifying women. Doll leaned towards these men, listening to their news. As she turned back to inquire of her instructor the true status of Ahab in the community and in the Hierarchy of Hell, she found to her great sorrow that he was gone.

118

At the same time one of the barnyard fowls who the night before had suffered bitterly, being as he was a cock, struck a gallant attitude upon a heap of dung, and, lifting his head, greeted the coming day with a triumphant cock-a-doodle-doo. She heard the cocks on her own farm answer this challenge with distant fairy cries.

This was a new day, and with it came great hopes.

Later she was asked if she did not know that cocks crow at an earlier hour — for they generally begin before the light. Yes, this she knew. But her demon must have had the power to stay the crowing of the cocks, for he never remained later than the first cry from such a bird, yet often he stayed until the day was almost light — for instance, on that first meeting. It was light when he left, and yet no cock cried until he was gone.

Where did he go to?

He went back to Hell.

2

How Doll became a Servant to the Servant of Hell.

This fiend — this caco-demon — came to her again and yet again. But after his first visit there was a pause and it seemed likely that he might not come again. She thought daily to get his summons, either to Black Sabbath or to class of more instruction. Would he bid her mount a broom and fly to him? Against this emergency she went to Dame Cosset's, a broom-maker, and paid sixpence ha'penny for a new red broom that she might appear handsomely mounted before her lord. This broom she hid in her chamber. Likewise she hid rushes and clay for the devising of poppets, and glass, knives, pins, and needles, for the working of her master's will.

On the eighth night from the time of the Thumb fire, she heard close by the house the hooting of an owl — which she knew was no owl. And Hannah, too, recognized the falsity of that cry, for she started up, saying that Indians were about. That was at eight o'clock. At nine they heard again the crying of an owl, and the dog at the barn began to howl dismally. Hannah swore that it was the bonded boys playing tricks. By ten again the hooting of the owl, but Hannah slept. Doll Bilby got to her room, and, taking clothes and a pillow, made a dummy of herself which she thrust into the bed, thus to deceive Hannah if the woman should look about for her. Grasping her red broom, but not essaying to mount it, she ran joyously from the house, anxious to meet her god or the accredited messenger of that god.

She came out of the house and found the moon to be rising and the night to be of a dainty, delicate, springtime beauty. Birches twinkled in the moonlight; their slender trunks seemed to be the white limbs of nymphs. The grasses that her broom brushed were sweet with flowers. She ran up and down the pastures, along the fences, over the fields. She ran until she was like to drop, and then found him where hereafter she always was to find him — in an opening in birch woods, enthroned upon a tussock. In the flowery pasture land this spot which he had selected for himself was a darling fairy bower. The exact spot is known to this day, for Doll, on seeing the fiend, threw her red broom into the birch trees, thus marking the spot, for she never took it back with her. Five years later boys found it and, on being taken to Dame Cosset, the woman said yes, it was one of her own brooms, and indeed the very one she had once sold to wicked Bilby for sixpence ha'penny. It is noticeable to this day that cattle will not graze there, and that dogs coursing for rabbits will stop frozen at this place and howl;

yet so inferior is the good sense and righteousness of man to that of beasts, it has become a common tryst for lovers, who, in each other's arms, repeat with foolish laughter (and yet, it may be hoped, with some sensible fear) the story of how Bilby's wicked Doll there met and loved a demon. Then they will go by moonlight to the cellar hole of the Bilby house, and pick a little of the yellow broom which country people call witch's blood.

The demon Prince permitted the witch to kneel to him and let her kiss his feet (which were not cloven). She noticed how cold to touch he was — like the fiends and devils in old tales. But the big hands he put upon her head (she reverently kneeling) were warm as any man's, and this heartened her. So he welcomed her 'Fellowship Christian in.' Then he seated himself and permitted her to sit. At first the talk was of great dignity, but soon it was much like that of one gossip to another. He told her how his work had prospered him in Salem, in Boston, and how in Hartford. And how another fiend (but this one in shape of woman) worked in New York among the silly Dutch, as far north as Albany, and yet another (this fiend in the shape of a great tawny dog) in Virginia and the Carolinas.

'Ah,' cried Doll, 'how thankful I, or rather all of us witches roundabout the Bay Colony should be that you have deigned to appear to us in the shape of a true proper man.' The fiend laughed horribly, saying there had been much complaining among the wizards and the warlocks because he was but a man — not a wild free wanton wench like she of the Dutch country.

Then he asked her if she could come with ease to him on such nights as he should call her, and she answered yes, she could come to him, but she must always wait her foster mother's sleeping and then leave secretly by her own window. She begged him to cry no more as hooting owl, for this aroused suspicion — the woman guessing it to be a man's voice. At this he seemed angry, and said the cries she had heard were in truth no man's cries, for he had bade an owl to go about the house and hoot. He explained to her that, as man may not laugh convincingly upon command, neither may owl hoot. Still, for such clumsiness the owl must die. So they argued for a while, Doll pleading with him to spare the unfortunate owl, and in the end, going back on her early statements, she said the cry had not sounded like a man, but exactly like an owl, and that the creature had hooted amazing well. He agreed, therefore, to spare the owl and to send him often to call her out.

She was rejoiced and humbled to think that he, so great and busy a fiend, would find time to send for her again and again, and she confessed to him the unendurable loneliness, desolation, and despair of her life — especially since her foster father had died; how even Titus, who had once professed to love her, now fled in terror from her glance, fearing her witchcraft; how Mrs. Hannah dreaded her so she would not leave a combing of hair nor a paring of nail about the house, and also how this woman had butchered Gideon and her other creatures.

As she talked the fiend came close to her, soothing her with his hands upon her body. Then she suddenly stopped her rehearsal of sorrow, and for a moment she went in deathly fear, for she guessed what the fiend intended. Still, such was her wickedness, she also felt uplifted and glorified, and in the end, it were these feelings that conquered in her, for she entirely forgot or set aside Christian fears and Christian modesty. The fiend kissed her and told her to be of good heart, for of all the many witches he had met in his recent travels through New England, it was she he most fancied and she should be his paramour. So she consented, and thus came to be the servant of the servant of Hell.

3

A thought for a Wise Man. Is Beauty of Flesh a good or evil thing? And the opinions of pagan Antiquity as contrasted to our own THEOLOGY.

There is one quality in this world which men call goodness. This is the beauty of the spirit, and is from God and of God. There is another quality, which is beauty of the body, and from whence comes it?

The heathen Greeks, whom the Reverend Pyam Plover has suggested were but devil worshippers, believed these two things to be identical; that is, what is good is beautiful, what is ugly is evil. Yet need the thoughtful Christian but read history, or look about him to-day, to see that rather than identical these two beauties should be considered non-congruent or mutually antagonistic. All must have observed how often the most virtuous women have been of no great bodily beauty, and yet certain famous wantons have been blessed (or cursed) with bounteous

125

fleshly charms. One should but consider the
lives of Cleopatra, that Helen known as Helen
of Troy, Dido, etc.

Beauty of the body, in that it excites to lust
and evil thoughts, is wicked, but the sick, ugly,
maimed body, in that it excites the sweet and
gentle passion of pity, is from God. For this
reason modesty in the young, blooming, comely
female is of greater necessity than in the sick and
ancient.

But it is not alone in a consideration of the
needful and (in its proper place) decent female
body that one may observe how often Evil has
wormed its way into the hearts of humanity
under specious guise of Beauty. For when the
Devil would steal the soul of Bilby's Doll, he
showed her lavishly and in wanton profusion
such sights of pagan beauty no Christian, godly
woman may ever expect to see.

For her this seemly ordered earth, on which
we set our houses, in which we humbly plough
and delve — this quiet earth for her brake open
into a rare flowering. She saw the satyrs (close
by the salt marshes) gambolling upon mud flats.
In the morning she saw the goatprints of their
hooves. She heard nymphs sing all night in

trees. She saw birch trees in the moonlight spun out of solid silver, and those common flowers, which by day (and in the sight of God) are but buttercups, turned into glittering jewels which by their very brilliance frightened her. Even that fiend the Devil sent to her was handsomer far than any mortal man might be. He was lovely to the eye, and his touch was as the touch of fire. The strength of his arms was beyond that of mortal men (who are born but to praise God and die). So was every moment that she spent with him a moment of ecstasy. How can mortal man contend with fiends in the love of woman? Have they such unholy power to arouse passion?

It is well known that no woman who has ever accepted an infernal lover may content herself with the ruck of men — such seeming, after the love of Hell, but pale, unsubstantial shadows. And the same may be said the other way over, for men, it is said, who have known nymphs, elves, or succubi, will long for them all their lives, eschewing the feeble impuissant arms of women.

So it is an established fact that Beauty that delights the eye is more often a curse from

Lucifer than a blessing from God. Let the reasonable and righteous man content himself with that which is plain and seemly — whether it is a church or wife or horse or land that he considers. Let him not yield to the delights of the eye, but rather to the beauty of goodness, piety, etc., which burns from within.

4

Some remarkable Wonders of an Invisible Kingdom.

For fairy women came to her by night, whispering . . . 'Get up . . . get up . . . get up . . .'

Strange hands plucked at her bedclothes, pinched or patted her.

Although her window was fast shut, once a great scaled and hairy arm came in by that same window, and she trembled. Now the arm grew to three times, four times, the length of human arm. She saw it sweep the room with a blind and scythe-like motion. It searched for her. She remained still. Then it was gone as miraculously as it had come.

There was a vast animal that rubbed nightly against the house, sniffing and blowing.

A monster (she thought it a demon) treaded the roof-tree by night.

Such was her appreciation of these awful and yet to her (coming from him she chose to accept as God) pleasing sights, she scarcely slept, being more awake by night than day, for at night she could hardly lie upon her bed nor close her eyes. She was forever staring and listening, listening and staring. With the crowing of the cock these disturbing visions retreated to that same Hell in which they had their geneses.

Sometimes she floated forth without volition, as on a certain night when she cried out, 'Master, command me and I will come.' Then far away and from the midst of the moonlight, she heard fairy women cry, 'Get up . . . get up . . . get up . . .'

'Then I will,' she said. Of a sudden her body was filled with lightness and (at first maintaining her horizontal position) she was elevated from off her bed. Thrice around the room she floated and, looking down, she saw her own vacant body as it lay still and flat as any corpse. 'If I am going out to walk wet fields,' she thought, 'I should put on slippers.' Then the red slippers Mr. Bilby once had bought her in Boston appeared upon her feet. She floated through the window, but once this was cleared she was set in vertical position. However, she felt no contact with the grass, and she took no steps. She floated on.

The moon was big upon the hills. The night air shook ravishing perfumes from the flowers and new leaves. The air was full of birds' songs (although it was dead of night), of voices, strange music, laughter. She floated on. The silver birches twinkled and bowed to her. Her name was called by a thousand little voices. A million gleaming eyes watched her. At last she was thus conveyed to the fiend, who was seated upon a hillock, as on a throne. He raised her up when she would prostrate herself to him. He bade her have no fear, for, although in Hell he was indeed a great prince, upon earth he was as mortal man and her true love.

In the morning, when she awoke in her own bed, she believed that the adventure of the night had been but another dream. She drew her body from between the sheets, and set her feet upon the floor. Upon her feet were the red slippers, and they were wet. Upon the sheets were green stains from the grass crushed beneath her feet.

Now could she know truth from dreams and dreams from truth.

5

We are informed that there is no marriage nor giving in marriage in Heaven, but in Hell it well may be otherwise.

She never saw her fiend by day. He came at dead of night. He went by cock crow (yet, as already pointed out, sometimes delaying this same crowing). He ruled by love and not by terror. She gave him soul and body, both as act of impious homage, and of true love. So a month wore away — the month of June.

At every turn and in every way he comforted and charmed her. She confessed to him how greatly she dreaded that day, which he said must now soon come, when he would be summoned back to Hell. She begged him to take her with him — for without him she had no use for this dull earth. She begged him to slay her now, and thus, her spirit released, she would take her way with him to Hell, and there live with him, once more with her parents — whom the French burned in Brittany. So she fitted his hands to her throat. He would not. He only promised her again and again that when she lay dying he himself would come to her once more, and stand at her bed's head. He promised her a short life, and life everlasting.

So this young woman, who had often shown a need for true religion, found great comfort in a false one. It was a fiend that fed, it would seem, her soul's hunger. By him and by the hopes of Hell she was comforted, as the true Christian is by his Lord and the hopes of Paradise. She became reconciled to life, to death, to adversity, loneliness, and despair.

There was no problem that he could not answer for her, no doubt he did not lay. For instance, she was distressed to think that when her true life should begin (that is, when she died and entered Hell) she would not see the kind foster father, but would undoubtedly encounter his disagreeable wife. No, explained the demon, she was wrong, for he knew that Jared Bilby was already there, well and at peace. He had committed mortal sin by saving her when a child, for she was already a witch, and it is mortal sin to save a witch. 'But at the time he did not know I was a witch. I do not think he ever believed it.' The demon said that made no difference. Mortal sin was mortal sin, but Satan, grateful to him for saving the life of Doll, had never carried out the cruel sentence which had been meted out to him at the Awful Judgement Seat. Doll wanted to know what this sentence was. He said it was of so revolting a nature he could not tell her. His words made her hate Jehovah, and she felt Satan was a kinder 'god.'

The demon went on to assure her that Mrs. Hannah would undoubtedly be given place in Heaven. She was a pious woman, always at meeting, lecture, and prayer. There were already millions of just such vixens singing miserable psalms, badly out of tune, about the golden streets. If she did in some way get sent down to Hell, he promised they would all get together and make it hot for her. They couldn't endure such ugly scolds in Hell. Doll was surprised. 'She is not ugly. She is remarkably handsome.' The devil was surprised. He said he had supposed from what he heard that she must be very ugly.

There was now only one thing with which she could vex herself, for her demon comforted her at every turn. Sometimes as he held her in his arms she moaned a little and pulled away. He begged her to tell him. He was her true love. Let her tell him and he would help. Then she told him that she knew that upon occasions fiends do actually marry mortal women. He laughed at her, and tried to turn her fancy from such homely thoughts. She would not be turned. He said witches and women talked alike, and yet he did not refuse to marry her.

With the commendable and proper thought of marriage in her head, she sought out Goody Greene (whom she had seen but little of late). She walked with her through the woods, helping her gather that bitter flower which the Indians call the jug-woman's-baby. The old woman was tired and the two sat upon a stone. From where they sat Doll could see the birch woods, the rough pastures, where by night she met her devil.

'Dear Goody, tell me as you used to tell the story of the goblin or infernal who came to a maid's window on a May eve and wed her in a respectful and seemly manner. Why cannot devils always do so? It is sad to think that a loving wench — betrayed by love — may become but the doxy of the devil.' She was near tears — although now she never had tears to shed.

The old woman told the story of Fair Jennifer of Bageley Wood. She had a demon lover — a black and scaly fellow, cold to touch as serpent or any ice or iron. He came to her window three times, calling her to get up and come to him. She lay disobedient upon her bed. Then on the third occasion he entered her chamber by the chimney hole, bearing in his hands green branches, and he was dressed in green leaves. Jennifer and the demon walked around and around the bed. He promised to be her loving husband until death, to avenge her of her enemies, and she promised to be his obedient wife until death and after death, and to deny God and Christ Jesus. Then upon the hearth she made him a cake, and in the cake they put blood drawn from the veins of both their arms. They ate this cake and were man and wife. His name was Karlycuke. But Fair Jennifer of Bageley Wood has been dead three hundred years. Such a thing cannot happen to-day. Doll thought otherwise, but kept her own counsel. Nor was she wrong.

On the way back to the hut on the waste land, Doll asked her how it was she could always remember these old stories. The woman said she had told them many, many times. 'To other children, as once you told them to me?' 'Yes,' she said, 'to other children.' Then she set down her basket and put her arms about Doll. She said once she had a son, but she would say no more of him and Doll guessed he was a long time dead.

One night, a night of full moon, Doll woke and found the fiend there in the room beside her bed. He signed her to silence, but Doll, who had many times by night stolen out of the house, knew that Hannah in her attic room slept soundly. All that the black and scaly fiend did for Jennifer, he now did for his love, and more. He set his imp upon the bedpost for a witness, and on the whole nothing could have been more seemly. There was no hearth in Doll's chamber. They could bake no cake. He pricked his wrist and her wrist, and each drank a little from the other's veirs. This slight cut upon her wrist never healed, as would a normal cut. It was red and angry to the day she died. Thus does Nature (which usually essays to heal) shrink from the lips of Hell.

It was the last of June, and the summer solstice (for on that day he married her) was passed. The leaves broadened into summer and the night air no longer held the rhapsody of spring. Now Doll had always known that he must leave her, but it hurt her to find that he could go without farewell. She comforted herself with the memory of his sweet love and her hopes for the future.

6

The Quenching of three Evil Firebrands.

There were hanged upon a spit of mud in the tidal waters of the Charles at Boston, on the tenth day of July, 1671, three pirates, long wanted for their unparalleled offences. These three, Black Pig Murch, Ben Bottle, and the Bloody Shad, had been taken into custody some two months earlier, but, having escaped their guardians, separated each to his own hiding. By agreement they came together again upon the second of July, thinking the hunt to be up and that they could get a pinnace and sail south to safety. So all three were taken together, but the fourth, Calico Jack, was never taken. Being duly indicted and tried, these fine rogues were found guilty of many homicides, robberies, and cruel acts of mayhem upon the high seas, so were condemned to hang.

Justice was done upon their bodies, and in due time (after the corpses had hung in chains some weeks, serving as due warning to others, especially to seamen) these bodies were buried in mud, close to the place where they had died.

Sic transeunt maleficii mundi!

CHAPTER VI

1

A Trap is set for two Tender Souls

DOLL never thought the demon would wait until her death-bed to come to her. Every moonlight night and every sunny day she looked for him and thought, 'Perhaps this day or this night he will come to me.' She always wore even quite commonly her prettiest, most worldly clothes, and she kept her shaggy black hair as neat as she was able. She thought, 'He sees me always, everything I do, everything I wear,' and she kept herself comely for him. She guessed he even knew her thoughts, and so she dedicated them to him.

In her own chamber she daily worshipped and prayed to Satan, as the fiend had taught her; that is, by foul blasphemies, such as the reversal of the Lord's Prayer, etc. She even wrote little hymns to Satan and entuned them for him. She felt that she should be about some harm, such, for instance, as the bewitchment of the godly, but she received no command, so she did, for some time at least, no devilment. She was happy and grew sleek.

The widow was already courted by three men, all reputable widowers and church members. Now that the windows were opened and Doll sang as she worked, and her own mind was taken up with her suitors, she did not fear her so much. Each went her own way.

Doll had always shown a dawdling and trifling attitude towards honest labour. And in this offence Bilby had encouraged her. For he had had her out in the woods and the fields (where there was nothing a young female could do) with himself, instead of leaving her at home to serve Hannah, as would have been more proper.

Now that he was gone, Doll still continued in her childish and frivolous wanderings. She often sat herself on the stone fence by the willow brook which divided the lands of the Bilbys and the Thumbs. The bonded boys upon the farm said they often saw her sitting upon the stone fence and feeding small rotten apples to Ahab (whose ferocity now had grown hideous). Yet this girl patted him freely, talking to him, laying her face against his cheek, and all these attentions Ahab accepted of. She wished him for her familiar, but the creature (so she told Mr. Zelley) would never do one of the things she asked of him, except to pursue and render ridiculous young Thumb.

Mrs. Thumb heard that her black bull was often down on the boundary with Bilby's Doll. She asked that he be penned, for she guessed that Doll was at the bottom of Ahab's remarkable dissatisfaction in Titus. She wished the bull withdrawn from the young woman's influence. By so doing and thus making these fields by the willow brook safe to cross, she did great harm to her own household, for now it was Labour and Sorrow who came daily (if they could) to see Doll. Undoubtedly she had been waiting for the twins to come and play with her. She must have seen in these weak and disobedient little girls fit matter for her to work upon to the further enlargement of the Kingdom of Hell. For she lay in wait there, and finally they came to her. They came slyly. No one at first knew they came, and they played at ungodly games, furtively, where no one of either house could know. Thus passed September, and October, and the half of November.

2

The Horrible Example of the Thumb Twins, or to what a Pass Disobedience may bring a Child.

Doubtless some who read these words will recall how in childhood they were brought to obedience and wholesome respect for authority by hearing a mother, or grannie, or aunt, or servant tell them the awful story of the Thumb twins, and to what their disobedience brought them. It is true that these children had never been well, and for them to fall from health to point of death was not a long fall. Nor when one considers what good use has been made of their example, and how many other children have learned decent docility from their story, can one wholly regret the incident which occurred as follows.

On the twentieth day of November (the day had been a mellow, warm, yellow day) the disobedient Labour and Sorrow went to the willow brook, and there found, as they hoped to find, the witch-woman awaiting them. She was all in fine scarlet as her fancy was. The children said they dared not stay and play — their mother had sent them to Goody Greene's to buy mints. She would wonder if they did not return within

141

the hour. They said (a long time later) that Doll smiled at them in a terrible fashion and suggested to them that what their mother wanted was of no importance. But the twins for once were mindful of their good mother's wishes. They said again they could not stay. They had only come to tell her that they could not stay. 'Well, take that then,' said the witch, and angrily tossed across the brook and to their feet two dolls that she had contrived out of corn husks and pumpkin seeds. So she went away, and the twins went to Greene's.

They came home again and they were late as usual, or rather as always, for they were dawdling, mischievous children. Their mother was angry with them. She could not whip nor even shake them. She dared not, they were too feeble. She put them to bed without their dinner and there they lay to supper-time, talking and whispering, laughing to each other. She bade them get up for supper. They would not, but lay in their bed. No one thought further of them until morning. The truth is that, having no dinner and no supper, they grew hungry and so they ate the dollies, which were made mostly of pumpkin seeds. The pumpkin in all its parts, even the seeds of it, is wholesome food. It could not be this that sickened the children, yet from that day they sickened.

For forty-eight hours they were afflicted in their stomachs. This passing a little, an even more grievous malady seized their bowels, which seemed to rot away. Their very bones gave out from within them, refusing to support their weight, etc. They pined, would not eat because of the pain they were in. First it was 'My belly, mamma, oh, my belly!' and the next, 'My throat, mamma!' or 'My head, mamma, my miserable bowels! My vitals are decaying within me.' These frightful pains were the result of their disobedience, for if they had done as bidden — that is, if they had eschewed the young woman and received no presents from her — they never would have so suffered.

They had thus sickened and suffered for a week, and then Mrs. Thumb, putting fresh linen upon their bed, found, between bed and wall, all that remained of the pumpkin-seed poppets. It was plain that these two poppets were intended to represent the twins. They were all but identical, yet was the one (Sorrow) plumper than the other (Labour). They had dark eyes, made from little buttons, and light hair fashioned from corn silk. In this respect they simulated the brown eyes and yellow hair of the twins. The one was tied about the waist with a red rag, and the other with a blue, and it was thus in these two colours Mrs. Thumb habitually dressed them.

The twins gaped at their mother as she found these things, and their eyes were guilty eyes. She asked them from whence came these dollies. They swore they did not know. Perhaps a cat had brought them in. They were sure a cat had brought them in. Their mother told them they were lying and they said nothing. She said she would shake them, and they said that they were far too sick, and Labour offered to fall into a

144

spasm. Well, if they would not tell from whence
these things were, would they tell who it was that
had eaten out the pumpkin seeds that had made
their vitals. The twins responded heartily, yes,
it was they themselves who had eaten up the
vitals. The woman cried out in anguish, 'My
children, oh, my poor children, it is your own
vitals that you have eaten, God help us all!'
And she rushed from the sick-room, weeping,
wringing her hands, screaming to her husband,
her son.

For three days the twins would not say from
whence were these poppets. Their mother
fancied it was old Goody Greene had given them,
because she knew that the girls had been to her
evil hut on the very day they sickened. Now
Greene, as well as Mr. Kleaver, had been called
in every few days to advise in the care of the
twins. Mrs. Thumb was enraged to think that
she had thus allowed the woman access to her
darlings. But Widow Bilby told her to look to
Doll, for she knew that she had in her own room
pumpkin seeds with red and blue rags, and corn
silk. She warned her, 'Look to Doll.'

In her heart the woman was convinced that
her little ones suffered from witchcraft. Mr.

Zelley, who showed at that time a most stubborn disbelief in such infernal manifestations, or perhaps wishing to protect the wicked, pooh-poohed the idea. Mr. Kleaver also said that such wasting fevers were indeed far from rare. By the New Year he promised the twins would be well or in their coffins. He himself had seen no signs of demoniacal possession.

The woman asked the children — for who should know as well as they? At first they stoutly denied the idea and then weakened, admitting that it was possible. When their mother pressed them further, they put their heads under the bedclothing and remained mute. The mother decided to spy upon them to see if between themselves they might not prove more honest.

She told them she was going abroad. And she left the door of the chamber open into the fire-room. Having bid them farewell and slammed the front door, she returned on tiptoe to the stool she had set herself behind the chamber door. There she listened. They talked little and but casually. And then at last Labour said, 'I wish we had not eaten the pretty poppets Mistress Dolly made us. I wish we had them to play with.' So she knew that in truth the poppets were from Doll. Nothing more of consequence was said.

That very night, however, they woke up the whole house, screaming that a great tawny cat had come down the chimney and had sat upon their chests, kneading its paws and purring most hideous. Father, mother, and brother flew to them. They saw no cat, but there were two red fresh scratches on the face of Labour. Their father reproved them for their fancies, reminding his wife how since early childhood they had been subject to night fears. The children were ashamed. They put their heads under the bedclothing. From then on, however (when their father was not present), they often spoke of this cat, and suggested even more horrible visions that came to torment them. Every day their plight was more piteous.

Almost in the middle of December, close to the shortest day of the year, the woman sat by her hearth, pondering these things. She was determined to find the truth for herself. Husband, doctor, and minister were all wilfully blind.

The children lay sick in the next room, and often seemed like to die. The one said to the other, 'She will come again to-night.' At the word 'she' the woman pricked her ears. It was only of the cat they had spoken before, and this cat they called 'he.' The child said, 'She will bring her baby and let us play with it.' The other said, 'Oh, I hope she will not come. Although she seems kind to us, I am afraid that it is she who hurts us, for God knows we are bewitched.' (She vomited a little.)

The woman went to the door, saying, 'Pretty pets, who comes to you, and of whom is this baby?' She spoke quietly. They hid their heads and would not answer. The woman went again to the fireplace and listened. 'I think,' said one, 'it is her cat that comes to hurt us,' and the children whispered together. The woman trembled with excitement. She did not go immediately to the children! instead she sat close by the fire and listened. Sorrow said, 'And the little black man with the little black hat . . .' She could hear no more. But later Sorrow was saying, 'Little people came, no bigger than my finger. They ate a little feast of honey and suet, served out to them in acorn cups — like those Mistress Dolly makes for us . . .' And later, 'There was a tiny queen. She looked just like

148

Mistress Dolly, only smaller, a Mistress Dolly you could put away in a teacup, and her baby was no bigger than a thumb nail...' The mother now felt she had proof. She hurried to her children, begging them to tell her all. Could Mistress Dolly, then, shrink no bigger than a poppet? And who was the little black man? At first the children would not speak, but, as was usual, stubbornly hid their heads.

She wept and prayed over them, begging them to be frank with her, for, if it were only known who bewitched them and how, they might be cured. As it was they would grow sicker and weaker, and finally languish and die. They protested they did not want to die, and began to weep and cast themselves about. And at last they confessed to everything (but in the midst, Labour was thrown into a grievous fit). They told how it was Bilby's Doll had given them the poppets; how she came to them every night — not cruelly using them, but amusing and diverting them. 'And she had with her a book...' said Sorrow. 'My children, my poor miserable children ... was it a black book, and have you signed?' Yes, it was a black book. No, they had not signed.

Then the pious woman got out the Bible, and she made them kiss it and swear that no matter how ill-used they were, or how delicately they were tempted by the witch, they would remain fast-sealed to God and not sign away their souls to Hell — no matter if devils did come and pull their vitals up by the roots and run needles through their eyeballs and brain-pans. The children, lamenting, shrieking, and yet for once obedient, promised and swore as they were bid.

3

A Hideous Malady and a Bridle for it.

From the day mentioned above Doll made no further pretence at kindness, for she began to come to these twins in hideous and cruel aspect. The deacons of the Church, the elders, the con-stables, the neighbours, took turn and turn about, in praying with them. These good words would often frighten away the witch, with her black book and infernal troop, and the little ones would rest a little or even sleep.

At last was the godly father of the haunted children convinced that this was witchcraft. He or his son Titus sat night and day with a bastard musket in the hand and a silver bullet in it.

At last was Mr. Kleaver convinced, and the doctor from Salem was convinced, and Mr. Increase Mather from Boston was convinced, that here at Cowan Corners was being enacted the most heinous and wicked witchcraft ever practised by any one in the New World. Here was indeed a witchcraft. Where was the witch?

Doll Bilby claimed that at this time she knew the children to be sick, but because week in and week out no one spoke to her (she went no more to Meeting) she had not guessed they were bewitched nor that she was talked about. She said she was sorry for what she mockingly called 'her little friends.' So she made a junket, and a fowl being killed she made a broth and put expensive cloves and nutmegs in this broth. She laid these things in a basket and asked the youngest of the farm servants to go present this basket to the Thumb twins, but not to say from whom it was.

When the mother saw the basket she cried out. Upon the handle of the basket in pretty Indian fashion were strung blue beads, identical with those the poor little wretches had but lately spewed forth. The children set up a great clamour at the sight of this food, for, although so hard to tempt, this particular food they would eat. She consulted Mr. Zelley (it was the last time she ever consulted him). He said it was good food and let the children eat. So they ate and quickly fell to sleep. That night they woke in horrid writhing fits, and almost died. Not only did they see Doll Bilby as she floated about over their bed, but Deacon Pentwhistle saw her and three others. Also Mr. Minchon, on going to the horse barn to get out his horse and ride home (for it was late), was bitten mysteriously in the arm. Lot Charty, a poor boy, that same night saw a fiery rat, and he said to this same rat, 'Who are you?' The rat said, 'I am who I am.' And he said, 'Whom serve you?' And the creature replied, 'I serve Hell and the will of Bilby's Doll.' Then with a clap like thunder he was up the fire hole.

A woman by the Ipswich Road that selfsame night sat nursing a feeble babe. She said the room grew light and there before her stood an awful female form. She never had set an eye upon Bilby's Doll, but by description she knew that this was she or her apparition. The child in her arms gave a great screech and the female form made off. Then (although it was midwinter) to the mother's apprehension, lightning came and struck the babe, squeezing it flat as a plank so it died.

Doubtless there were many devils abroad. The blessed God permitted their escapement from Hell that they might give bodily confutation to all atheists who should say 'there is no God.' So must ever the Prince of Lies and his servants serve the will of God. Because of the powers of an invisible Kingdom manifested in the years 1671–72, the churches were gorged with the pious and the entire community awoke to an awful realization of the potency of God.

Non est religio ubi omnia patent. (Which might be translated, Where there is no mystery there is no religion.)

All in all there seemed no proof lacking that Cowan Corners and more particularly the Thumb twins were suffering from a cruel demoniacal tormentation. Mr. Kleaver and the Salem doctor, the deacons. the elders, Captain Buzzey, the marshal, and others gave affidavit in writing to the magistrates that the woman Bilby was a witch of provable perversity and that she should be set in jail. Mr. Zelley alone among all the men of standing had nothing to do with the signing

and drawing-up of this paper. In fact, such was
his strange, distrait, and heretical attitude, no
one asked him to assist. Already it was bruited
abroad that he was a man to be looked at, for,
after all, have not some of the most potent wizards done their blasphemies under a cloak of
piety?

So Captain Tom Buzzey, of the Train-Band
troop (and he was also sheriff), taking two constables with him, rode to the house of Widow
Bilby and there served warrant upon the young
woman. She showed neither surprise nor terror,
but looked up at her captors fearlessly. She
wanted to know of what she was accused. She
was primarily accused of afflicting the Thumb

twins. Why, then she was as innocent as a babe unborn. She would have explained to the sheriff that she had been the friend of these little ones ever since they could toddle. The sheriff told her that all were agreed that they were bewitched. If not she, who was it? Then she became confused and in the end said, 'It was the work of *another witch*,' thereby denying all and confessing all.

Captain Buzzey, as he had been instructed, searched her chamber and the house. He did not find the pumpkin seeds, corn husks, etc., etc., that Widow Bilby said the girl kept under her bed to work evil out of. It is likely the young woman really did know that her name was talked about and had rid herself of them.

She rode upon a pillion back of Captain Buzzey. A great jeering crowd had gathered to see her off to Salem jail. Widow Bilby laughed loudly from where she stood in the crowd between two of her suitors, 'You've got it now, you jade, you jade!' she cried.

Captain Buzzey said the girl bowed her head and he heard her whisper, 'He has not abandoned me. My god, my god, protect me and save me.' Thinking that she was referring to our Lord Jesus Christ and to the true God, he, in his heart, pitied her. She begged Captain Buzzey to hurry. 'Oh, for pity's sake take me out of this crowd.' He clapped spurs to his stallion, and the young horse, in spite of his double load, put off at a gallop. The day was a winter day, crisp and cold, and the snow was fresh and spotless under the horses' hooves. So at a tremendous pace the cavalcade of armed men and the one prisoner passed through dark woods and by a winter sea. They rode for six miles and came to Salem, where again they encountered angry faces, hoots, gibes, and threats of instant death.

That night she lay upon straw and without a mattress. The dungeon was so cold the water froze in the jug. She could not sleep for cold, but spent hours upon her knees in prayer (as the jailor later reported), yet now it is known it was to her demon or to Satan that she prayed. At last a heavenly quiet descended upon her and she slept.

Concurrent to her jailing, the Thumb twins were a little eased in their misery. It would seem that the witch had been put to fright at the fear of bodily incarceration and pain, and that she had diminished the force and malignancy of her spells.

CHAPTER VII

1

JUSTICE *arrives. She will not be stayed nor thrown from her scent, although the morning wears slowly and some fear* JUSTICE *will be balked.*

On the twenty-seventh day of December, 1672, Judge Lollimour and Judge Bride, of the Court of Assistants, Boston, entered with pomp into Salem. They were escorted by the Boston marshal, by constables, aides, etc., in full regalia. This pretty cavalcade drew rein by the horse-block of the Black Moon, where ordinarily preliminary hearings were conducted.

Judge Bride (this was the great Judge Bride) said to Judge Lollimour, his colleague, 'Sir, what will we do with this great crowd gathered hereabout, waiting to hear the findings of Justice?'

'Sir,' said Judge Lollimour, 'the tap-room of the Black Moon could not accommodate one fifth of this great multitude. Let us move on to the Meeting-House.'

After them straggled the populace of some five villages — yes, and learned men, elders, doctors, jurists, etc., out from Boston. The crowd was black with the gowns of the clergy.

Every seat in the Meeting-House was quickly taken. The aisles were filled. Body pressed close to body, rendering breathing difficult. In this way a stale heat was engendered, and a fear, and an expectation. One said to another it was a fatal day. Some would have left if it had been allowed them, but the room being filled the Judges ordered the constables to permit neither egress nor entry. They feared a milling about and a turmoil that would be a detriment to the dignity of the Court.

The magistrates were set in great chairs before the pulpit. At their feet were pallets whereon the sick children should be laid when their time came to testify. The constables pulled a table (a heavy oak table) close to the magistrates. Upon this the accused should stand in the sight of all men — yes, and in the sight of God.

Certain men cried out, 'Make way! Make way!' and in came Captain Buzzey and the prisoner. She looked most wild and shaggy and of a touchingly small size. Captain Buzzey lifted her to the table set for her, and then, addressing the Court, showed true warrant for her arrest and swore that as commanded he had diligently searched the house for poppets, images, etc.; having found what he found, he now produced these things in the bundle which he laid at their honours' feet.

Judge Bride, looking about him at the many black-robed clergy, said, 'Gentlemen of the ministry, who among you officiating in these parts is senior?' He was told Mr. Zelley was senior in these parts, but that the famous Mr. Increase Mather was present. 'Sir,' said Judge Bride, 'will you, Mr. Zelley, offer up a prayer?' Mr. Zelley prayed, begging God to discover evil where there was evil and innocency where there was innocency. He prayed that the prisoner confess if she might be guilty, but if she were innocent, God strengthen her not to confess merely to save her life. To this prayer the magistrates gave fervent amen.

Judge Lollimour thus addressed the prisoner at the bar: 'You understand, Doll Bilby, whereof you are now charged, that is, to be guilty of sundry acts of witchcraft, more specifically the wasting and afflicting of twin sisters, Labour and Sorrow Thumb. What say you to it?'

'I am as innocent as the babe unborn.'

'You are now in the hands of authority and, God helping, you shall have justice, and the afflicted shall have justice. May God help us all.'

Then Judge Lollimour called on many witnesses. He called on Mr. Kleaver the surgeon, and the older doctor from Salem whose name was Bunion. He called upon the Thumbs and upon Widow Bilby. This latter woman showed such spite and malice in her testimony that Judge Bride frowned upon her and reproved her. Thus, instead of hurting the accused, she helped her, for the Judges felt some pity for the tousled, wild child (she seemed but a child) perched upon the table in the sight of all men — yes, and in the sight of God.

Mr. Zelley was called. He was a bony man of fifty years, and his hair was white. In contrast to the big fine presence of Mr. Mather and many another clergyman then present, he seemed a poor thing; that is, uncertain, ill at ease. He spoke in a low voice, saying how good had been this young woman as a child. How in earliest womanhood she had shown a most exemplary piety. How she was often at her prayers, and came to him for religious comfort, etc. As he spoke, he twisted his hands in his sleeves as a boy might.

Then he said in a defiant voice that the girl had since childhood endured the most cruel abuse from her foster mother — that is, from this same Widow Bilby, who had but lately been heard. This last statement had much weight with the Judges, who thereafter did not permit Widow Bilby to testify, or, if they did, they took her words with knowing glance. By this dismissal of Hannah they also dismissed the earlier tales of Doll's witchcraft. Although they heard how the green fruit of Hannah's womb was blasted, how she had suffered a wretched and unaccountable illness, it was evident they were not impressed — rather were they bored. To the death of Mr. Bilby they listened with more attention, questioning a number (especially Mr. Kleaver and Mr. Zelley) with some pains. When they heard that the dying man with his last breath denied any witchcraft, they would not permit Hannah to explain how it may be that an evil spirit enter a corpse and then cry out.

At noon, while they ate their bloaters and drank their rum punch at the Black Moon, the barmaid heard Judge Bride say to Judge Lollimour that it was easy to see through the whole miserable affair. *In primo:* This rustic town was so tedious they had to patch up an excitement — he would begin seeing devils himself if he lived there. *Secundo:* This jealous, scolding widow

was at the bottom of it. *Tertio:* The wench indeed looked like a goblin, and, no matter how pious a life she might lead, village gossips would always speak ill of her — especially, as in her own ungodly way she was a pretty mouse. *Quarto:* They would both of them be back in Boston within the three-day, the case being dismissed and the local people reproved for their gullibility. Said Judge Lollimour, 'Sir, we have not as yet seen these afflicted children.' Judge Bride said, 'Blah,' draining the last of his rum punch.

2

From Noon to Sundown rages a famous battle, with Righteousness and Justice on the one hand and Witchcraft and Evil upon the other.

On the afternoon of the same day, Doll Bilby was set again upon the table. The crowd within the Meeting-House was even greater than it had been in the morning. Many had not even gone out for dinner, so ravenous was their hunger to hear the findings of Justice and to observe the conduct of a witch.

Judge Bride: Once again are we assembled in the eyes of all men and in the eyes of God to administer justice as well as mortal man (a puny, weak, and miserable creation) is able. Mr. Mather, of Boston, sir, we beg your blessing and your prayers.

Then Mr. Mather prayed most decently, and as if in sight of God's most awful throne. To this prayer the Judges gave amen and bade the sheriff go and fetch the bodies of the Thumb twins, who should next be questioned. Out of the mouths of babes and sucklings wise men may be instructed, and an innocent child may speak

163

with greater knowledge than is given to the cloudy heart of maturity. Mrs. Thumb was asked to tell all she might concerning the health and humour of these twins since birth. These things she told. She told of the past-nature love her son Titus bore this woman now accused, and at the moment the sheriff entered and the cry 'Make way!' went up. After him was Deacon Thumb, and he bore Sorrow Thumb, and after him was Titus. He bore Labour Thumb. It was explained that the children were taken in fits at the threshold of the courtroom. They lay in a swoon as though dead, their faces green with pallor, their eyes closed. The bearers laid them on the pallets.

> *Judge Bride:* Titus Thumb, stand up and answer me. You see this woman who stands thus before and above you all. Now is she charged with crimes which, if proven, shall cost her her life, yet a year and a little more and she was your dear heart and you were about to wed with her. You have heard your mother say that this Bilby won you by wicked spells, that once she assumed the shape of Indian and you shot her through the heart — yet she did not suffer for it.

That again she perversely set upon you, tempting and staying you beyond the puny endurance of our sex, and you struck her a blow that would have killed an ox, yet *she* rose up unharmed. We have listened to some length of how violent and beyond the usual wants of nature was your desire for her. Your flesh fell away, etc. What do you now say? Are these things true?

Thumb: Sir, as God hears me, these things are true.

Judge Bride: There has been no enlargement upon fact?

Thumb: None.

Judge Bride: It does not seem to you that you mistook for enchantment what another would call lust? Possibly you are a young man of gross sensual nature, who might strike what he loved?

Thumb: God knows I am the least sensual of all men. I have never sought out women. Ask any here.

At that a girl was possessed and now a demon began manifestly to speak in her. The demon belched forth most horrid and nefarious blasphemies. The constable took her out. A dozen cried to the Judges, begging to vouch for the young man's purity. All were silenced.

Judge Bride: Thumb, I see your eyes avoid to look towards this young woman. Perhaps your heart regrets that you give testimony most like to lead her in the halter. Look upon her now. Is she not your enemy? Tell her she is a witch and that you wish her hanged for it.

Thumb (after a most tedious pause, looked to her feet): You are a witch.

Judge Bride: Better than that, louder and firmer. Come, you shall look upon her face. You shall not mock this Court.

Thumb: Sir, I cannot.

Judge Bride: What, are you still bewitched, or is it that you still love her and will not harm her?

Thumb: I love her. (He put his arm across his eyes. He wept.)

Judge Bride: Get to your chair again. How can you who love her give good and valid testimony? Get to your chair again. Your mother, she is made of sterner stuff. I see the children stir. They are about to be recovered to consciousness. Sheriff, cover the

face and body of the accused so that they
may not see her until the time comes.

Captain Buzzey took off his scarlet cape. It
was a good new cape that had cost him two
pounds. Within the month it rotted mysteriously, and the Assistants bought him another
one. With this scarlet cape he now covered
Bilby's Doll from head to foot.

Labour: Oh, for Christ's dear sake, sister,
where are we now? Oh, for God's sake . . .

Sorrow: Oh, my back, oh, my bowels!

The children aroused themselves a little, sat
up, and gazed about the court. Now it is noticeable that Judge Lollimour took to himself the
questioning of the children. The reason is he
had seven such at home, while the great Judge
Bride had none.

Judge Lollimour: Children, do not be afraid,
for is there none among us but wish you
well. You are only to speak the truth as
your good mother has taught you — the
whole truth, and nothing but the truth.

Sorrow (in loud, bold voice): There is one here
who does not wish us well. I can feel her
presence.

The Judge gave no heed, although many were

amazed that the child had not seen Doll, yet knew there was one there who did not wish her well.

Judge Lollimour: You have been strangely sick, and I see you are not well. What, think you, caused this sickness?

Sorrow: Oh, sir, have you not heard? We are bewitched. She gave us our own vitals to eat, and she comes at night and torments us.

Judge Lollimour: You say 'she,' yet half the world are 'she.' To whom do you refer?

Sorrow: I can't say her name, oh-oh-oh . . .

She gagged and went purple in the face, she clawed at her windpipe.

Labour: Oh, don't you see, don't you see, the witch has her by the throat? She won't let her answer. Oh, sir, she'll die. (The puny child struck the air above her sister's head.) Go away, you wicked witch, go away!

Judge Lollimour: Now that you are restored, I shall name some to you, and when you reach the name of her whom you think torments you, you shall make a sign. Abigail Stone, Sarah Black, Obedience Lovejoy, Alice May, Delilah Broadbent, Doll Bilby . . .

Then the afflicted did cry out, and fell back weak and dumb.

Judge Lollimour: So you accuse Doll Bilby, that she bewitches you, causing your sickness? What else does she do to you?

Sorrow: She will have us sign in the Black Book.

Judge Lollimour: Come, you contrive a fancy. I do not believe she comes with a black book. Tell me how.

Sorrow: She comes with devils and imps and hideous animals, and they torment us, pressing out our lives, sticking pins and knives into us, and while they torment us she presses close to us, bidding us sign her book. But we will none of her, and God helps us and will save us.

Judge Lollimour: You claim that this woman comes to you by night, bringing such with her as prick and torment you. How does she come, in her own proper form?

Sorrow: At first she would come as a great tawny cat, and then again as a pig, or as a mouse, and once I remember she came as a black dog. And she brings fiends with her, hairy little black men, and these tor-

169

ment us. Of late I think she comes only in her own proper form. Sometimes it is hard to tell, for she can at will assume any shape. And sometimes a hand puts into the bed amongst us and pulls at our vitals.

Judge Lollimour: When this woman came to you and offered you a book to sign (as you claim), what would she say?

Sorrow: She would say, 'Sign.'

Judge Lollimour: And no other word?

Sorrow: Sometimes she would say, 'Sign, or I'll squeeze your vitals for you.'

Judge Lollimour: But you, being good and Christian girls, would not sign?

Labour: Oh, sir, once a most awful and majestic voice spoke out, and I do believe it was the voice of God, and He bade us not to sign. Then the fiend flew away in a clap and did not return for a three-day.

Their mother said, yes, this was true. She herself heard the clap and it was three days before the affliction again commenced.

Judge Lollimour: And if you sign, what does she promise you?

Sorrow: Prettiest things to play with — little goats, no larger than a cat and a cat as

170

small as a kit, and brooms to ride on through the sky — and her own pretty babe to play with.

Judge Lollimour: And when you refuse to sign?

Sorrow: Oh, she pinches and torments us, or lets her fiends and familiars torment us. They but do her bidding and I do not think are as wicked as she. Once she set my father's great black bull Ahab upon us. He tramples us like to break our bones.

The mother interrupted to say, yes, this was true. The bull was a witch's familiar beyond good doubt, and they but waited the finding of the Court before they butchered him.

Sorrow: Sometimes the witch shakes us cruelly.

Thumb: Sir, it is true. Those small and puny girls were so shaken two strong men could not hold them in their beds.

Judge Bride: What, young Thumb, is this girl, even though proved a witch, so strong, she can best two strong men — how think you?

Thumb: Sir, I think the Devil helps her and he gives her strength.

Judge Bride: You who were once her lover —

you should know her strength. Was she then so brawny-strong those times you bundled her?

Titus was confused. He believed the Court to be against him. The congregation was angry, for bundling is a pleasantry for yokels, and no more likely to occur in Salem than in Boston, nor in the Thumb house than in the house of Bride or Lollimour. It was felt the Judge intended an insult. Some feared the magistrates might dismiss the whole case but from caprice. But Judge Bride was a godly man, who would not lift his nose from a scent until Justice herself was satisfied, although those who knew him best said he often seemed to pause and idly bay the moon.

Thumb: I never got such favour from her.

Judge Bride: One more thing you shall tell us, although you are not a likely witness. Is it true, as your mother has said, that you shot silver bullets up the fire hole, and that upon occasion you think you struck the accused?

Thumb: It is true, sir, but I shot only three silver bullets — these were buttons from my coat. My sisters cried, 'There she goes up the flue.' I fired where they pointed and they exclaimed that I had struck her on the wrist. Some here will tell you that there was indeed the next day a bullet-gouge on her wrist, nor has it yet healed — to this day. I saw it when you bade me look at her. You may see this mark yourself. Her apparition came commonly to afflict my sisters in an old black riding-hood.

Captain Buzzey said he had the very one with him in the bundle at their honours' feet. He took it out, and Labour and Sorrow both said, yes, it was the very one. Captain Buzzey held it up before the magistrates. It was riddled with bullet holes.

Captain Buzzey: Widow Bilby gave me this coat. See, it is burnt with fire, shot full of holes as a sieve, and still smells of soot from the Thumb chimney, and gunpowder from Thumb's musket.

A boy (crying out from the back of the court): I know that coat, sir, well.

Judge Bride: And who may you be?

The boy: Jake Tulley, bonded man to Widow Bilby, and I know that coat for the one our scarecrow has worn these three years, and but yesterday I saw the coat gone and the scarecrow naked. Mate and I (that is the other farmhand) often shot at it for practice. Why, it means nothing that it is full of holes.

Judge Bride: And are you and Mate such miserable poor shots you must press your pieces into the very belly of the scarecrow to be assured of your aim? Look, how the powder has burned the cloth.

The Judges took the coat up between them and discussed in low voices. Jake sat down in confusion.

Judge Bride: Mr. Kleaver, you have already given generously of your knowledge. You have told us in what way the maladies arising from witchcraft differ from those arising from the proper body — in other words, what are the differences between diseases inflicted by the Devil for wicked ends, and those by Jehovah for our own good. And you have told us how you came to recognize the case in hand as one provoked by art. Will you tell us further?

Mr. Kleaver: Invisible hands often clutched the twins by the throat. I have seen them.

Judge Bride: The invisible hands?

Mr. Kleaver: No. I have seen the throats. And I have also taken the needles, pins, and such from their flesh. These children have vomited strange things — fur, insects, glass, long hanks of hair — blue beads . . . (He stooped to the bundle at their honours' feet.) Sirs, here is the basket in which the young woman sent poisoned or possessed food to the afflicted — mark the blue beads on the handle. Three days earlier, the one of them spewed forth these blue beads I now take from my pocket — mark, gentlemen — they are identical.

Mrs. Thumb: There was never a bead like that before in my house.

She wept. The children screamed out in gibberish at sight of the beads, and fell back upon their pallets.

Judge Bride: Mark the children, Mr. Kleaver, are they now, in your opinion, possessed?

Mr. Kleaver: Not exactly possessed. (He whispered to the magistrates.) They are conscious of a malignant presence. They know the witch is in the room.

The twins: Oh, oh, oh, God help us, oh, oh, oh!

Judge Bride: Sheriff, uncover to us the accused. Now, children, stand up, if able, and look there at the table above you.

The room was filled with their piercing din. Labour fell in a fit, foaming, rolling her eyes. She was stretched out stark and dead. Sorrow flung herself in hideous terror upon the feet of the Judges, crying out piteously that they save her. Then she fell back stark and dumb. Judge Lollimour was touched by her plight, her fear, and the appeal she made to him. He raised her up, felt of her hands and face. They were dank with a cold sweat which both Judges knew no art could imitate. Her pulse scarce moved. Her tongue was tied in her throat. She could not speak. She looked up out of tortured eyes.

Mr. Mather: Here, sir, if ever, is demoniacal possession.

Judge Bride: Here is witchcraft — now to find the witch.

Mr. Mather: It has been proved an hundred times in English courts that a spell cast by a witch's eye must return to the witch's body — if the witch touch the afflicted.

Judge Bride: Sheriff, carry the body of this Labour Thumb to the prisoner. She shall touch her. We shall see. Observe. The child is utterly lifeless now.

Captain Buzzey: She has no pulse, sir.

Mrs. Thumb: Sir, sir, you have let her slay my child before my eyes. Oh, God, oh, God! . . .

Judge Bride: No one can say that this child knows who touches her. Sheriff, take her, alive or dead, to the prisoner.

Captain Buzzey took her up. The witch readily assented. She reached down and touched the child. The colour returned to the child's face. Captain Buzzey felt her pulse leap in her wrist. He felt her heart stir under her hand. The child turned in his arms, smiling prettily, as though in sleep. With a smile she woke. She glanced to the Judges, noted her sister (still in semi-trance). She smiled at her mother. Her eyes went up, and there on the table beside and above her was the awful vision of Bilby's Doll. With a wail of terror no art could simulate, she clung to Captain Buzzey. At that moment all in the courtroom realized how hideous had been her weeks of anguish. No one could so fear a person who had never done her harm.

Judge Bride: Lay the child upon her pallet —

and you, Sorrow, go you now and lie upon your pallet.

Sorrow (her tongue still tied): Gar, gar, gah, gah, gah.

Judge Bride: Labour and Sorrow, as you fell into these fits, tell me what occurred. Did a fiend or familiar come to torment you? Did the accused send her apparition to you, there before your very eyes — leaving her body, as it were, vacant upon the table? Tell us.

Now was Labour also taken with dumbness. All saw how the lower lips of the afflicted were sucked in, and the teeth were clamped down upon them. Mr. Kleaver essayed to break the lock on their teeth. He could not.

Widow Bilby: Look to the witch, look, look!

It was seen the witch bit her lip — thus locking the jaws of the children. Captain Buzzey struck her slightly, and bade her loose her lip. Then the children were released. They said it was her own devil came to them.

Judge Bride: Doll Bilby, I have asked several the meaning of the manifestation of evil, so recent among us. Mr. Kleaver and Mr. Mather have both explained it to the satisfaction of many — is it to your satisfaction?

Doll Bilby: I am an ignorant woman. I cannot explain.

Judge Bride: Now you are to talk freely, deny the truth of the statements which you have heard made, explain and elucidate for us — or, if you wish, you may confess.

She was silent.

Judge Bride: At least you can concur with the judgement of those wiser than yourself. At least say this, Was it or was it not a devil who tied the children's tongues for them?

Doll Bilby: That I do know — it was not.

Judge Bride: How do you know? No one else can claim to be so wise.

Doll Bilby: If it were a demon, I would have seen him.

Judge Bride: You have, then, so nice a sight you can see devils?

Mr. Zelley: May I speak?

Judge Bride: Speak.

Mr. Zelley: If this young woman could command a devil to serve her, would he then be so unmindful of her safety as to come into this court and work tricks so likely to hurt her cause?

Mr. Mather: Cannot God as well as this wretched girl or Satan command devils? Has it not been proved often and often that it sometimes pleases Him to suffer them to do such things in this world as shall stop the mouths of gainsayers and exhort a Christian confession from those who will believe only the most obvious of His truths?

Judge Bride: Bilby, give us your thoughts on the matter. These Divines have spoken wisely.

Doll Bilby: I think it was perhaps an angel — come to do me a mischief.

Judge Bride: Do angels come to do mischief to good and baptized women?

The defendant saw she was in difficulty. She twisted her hands in the folds of her gown. Then were the children afflicted.

Judge Bride: Bilby, if these are indeed your tricks, keep them for more seemly time. Constable, seize her hands. And if, as you suggest, these manifestations are the actions of angels, I pray God to spare us His angels until the Court is adjourned.

A woman was taken in a fit. She fell down laughing and sobbing, and was passed out through a window.

Judge Bride: Do you think those who are afflicted suffer voluntarily or involuntarily?

Doll Bilby: I cannot tell.

Judge Bride: That is strange; every one may judge for himself.

Doll Bilby: I must be silent.

Judge Bride: You have heard this morning two learned medici explain in what way witchcraft is like to resemble natural ailment, and in what ways it differs. Keep this counsel in your mind, and tell me what you would say of the illness of these children.

Doll Bilby: It would seem they suffer from witchcraft.

Judge Bride: So it would seem to many here. And where there is a witchcraft there must be a witch.

Doll Bilby: Yes.

Judge Bride: Where is that witch?

Doll Bilby: God knows I do not know. God knows I never hurt a child. I know of no witch that would afflict these children.

Captain Buzzey stood up. He said that when he and his men came to arrest this woman, now standing trial for witchcraft, he and his men heard her deny clearly the afflicting of the Thumb

twins, and yet she had said — most meaningly —
''Tis the work of *another witch.*'

Judge Bride: You shall explain this for us,
Bilby.

Doll Bilby: How shall I explain?

Judge Bride: Confess now, as you did then,
that you are a witch.

She was silent.

Judge Bride: Confess now, and your life shall
be spared.

She was silent.

Judge Bride: Confess now and turn against
these other witches — for it is possible that
many are about — and I swear to you your
life will be spared.

She was silent.

Judge Lollimour: Will the prisoner at the bar
recite the Lord's Prayer?

Doll began readily enough. As she spoke the
Holy Words, Mr. Zelley covered his face in his
hands, and made them with his lips as though
he would help her. She went on without chance
or mishap till she came to the last sentence,
which begins, 'Lead us not into temptation.'
She got no further. Mr. Zelley clenched his
hands until his knuckles went white. He turned

up his eyes to God. Then quickly she began and said, to the horror and consternation of all, 'Ever for, glory the and, power the, kingdom the, is thine for, evil from us deliver, but temptation into not us lead—Amen.' She did not know what she had done. She looked about with assurance. There was an incessant and horrid silence in the court. The Judges looked to each other. Clergyman looked to clergyman, then turned eyes to God. So was she utterly undone, but the Court was not yet satisfied.

> *Judge Bride:* You have responded to my colleague's request to the satisfaction of all, but there are some small matters yet to clear. Be of good heart, soon we will let you go. I see you are pale and distrait. Constable, see to it she does not fall from the table. What did you mean when you said the bewitchment of the Thumb twins was 'the work of another witch'?
>
> *Doll Bilby:* Sir, how can I explain?
>
> *Judge Bride:* There is nothing you cannot either confess to, or explain.
>
> *Doll Bilby:* Sir, I am confused and amazed.
>
> *Judge Bride:* Answer but a few minutes with frankness, and you shall go to your own

183

cell — we are not your enemies — open your heart to us.

She was mute.

Judge Bride: Be stubborn, and you shall stand there all night — yes, and the next day. Come, have you ever seen a devil?

She nodded her head.

Judge Bride: Ah, then you have seen a devil. Do not feel ashamed of that. Did not Christ Himself see Satan? Was not Luther often tormented by his presence? Some of the best of men have been the most foully pursued. Feel no shame, Doll Bilby. Speak out freely. When was it first?

Doll Bilby: I was a child in Brittany; my mother took me to see him in a great wood.

Judge Bride: An instructive and remarkable experience — and have you seen him since?

Doll Bilby: Last spring I saw him — he came to me again.

Judge Bride: In proper human form?

Doll Bilby: He came to me by night. Yes, he came in form of proper man. He wore seaman's clothes and with him was an imp — a black-faced imp with a long ringed tail. He wore this imp upon his bosom.

There was a commotion at the back of the hall.

Judge Bride: When did he come last spring to you?

Doll Bilby: The last night in May — the night the Thumbs' barn burned. Oh, sir, I am sick, let me go to my cell.

Captain Buzzey held her up.

A high, wild voice from the midst of the confusion: I will speak, sirs, you shall hear me.

Judge Bride: Who cries out?

Voice: I am Jonet Greene, the tinker's wife. There are things I know . . .

Judge Bride: Stand back, all, from the woman. Dame Greene, deliver yourself of these things.

The crowd drew back. Goody Greene, an old woman and of great dignity, was revealed to the Judges. Mr. Kleaver whispered to the Judges that she was an evil woman.

Goody Greene: This girl never saw a devil. She saw my own son Shadrach. He was wanted for piracy — Heaven help me, I hid him by day, but he prowled by night. He had a monkey, he wore seaman's clothes. He saw in my house the girl and lusted after her. I speak . . .

A man from back: Her husband says she lies — she never had no son.

Goody Greene: Believe me, for Christ's dear sake, believe me. I had a son and I hid him . . . but they found him just the same . . . God found out his sin. They hanged him; he was called the Bloody Shad.

The man: The woman's husband, sir, says she never had no son. Time has broken her memory.

Goody Greene: Husband, you are afraid. You coward, who will not confess to the son of your own loins, lest you come to shame — now is Doll indeed undone . . .

Judge Lollimour: The woman is lunatic. See how she rolls her eyes.

Judge Bride: Could you have had a son of which your husband knew nothing — why did you never speak of him to your neighbours? How can we believe your fables? You are lunatic.

Goody Greene: God help me! God help me . . . May God help Doll!

Judge Bride: Constable, throw out this ancient

— let her learn to be a sager hag — and her husband after her.

A confusion and clamour of tongues rose from all parts of the courtroom. Some wished to say what they knew of the Greenes; others had stories to tell of lunacy, devils, etc. And there was laughing and crying among women, and children wailed and would be taken home. Judge Bride stood up in a noble wrath.

Judge Bride: Clear the court! Clear the court! What, shall Justice find her house in Bedlam? Constables, pick up and carry out — if they are too weak to walk — the Thumb twins, and you, madame, who are their mother, go with them. Every one shall now be turned out into the snow except those who are the witnesses and proper officers of the law, and the six that I shall name. Mr. Increase Mather, Mr. Seth Dinsmore, Dr. Zerubbabel Endicott, Mr. Zacharias Zelley, Mr. John Wilson, and you, sir, also, Colonel Place Peabody. Gentlemen, the case shall be continued *in camera*. I beg of you few, however, to stay to the end.

3

From Sundown to black Night the battle continues. The Witch is thrown to confusion. Justitia triumphans. Deus regnat.

Now was the courtroom, empty and vast, silent as the grave. Only twenty remained in the room where a minute before had been many hundreds. The day had worn to sunset and the room was dark. Flares were lighted and candles were set where there was need. But the light of flare and candle made the far reaches of the room and the dark corners behind the scaffold even blacker. Such humanity as was present were huddled about the platform and the great chairs of the Judges. By candlelight Judge Bride glanced over the notes that he had taken, and by candlelight Titus Thumb looked to the witch upon the table. She stood there ghastly pale and like to swoon. Her eyes were round and struck terror to all. She did not look again to Titus, only to Judge Bride, whom she in her simplicity thought to be her friend.

Judge Bride bade the sheriff fetch a chair — a good chair with a back to it, for he said he saw that the accused was tired past human strength. Captain Buzzey got a chair. It was a great chair

similar to those in which the Judges sat. Judge
Bride had it placed on the platform between
himself and Judge Lollimour. The three sat
thus for a moment in silence, a judge, and next a
witch, and then a judge. So they sat in great
chairs and upon crimson damask cushions. The
witch's feet could not reach the floor. Judge
Bride gave her wine to drink from the silver
goblet set out for his own use. She drank the
wine and was grateful to him.

Little by little — tenderly — he questioned
her. And little by little she told him all. Of the
Thumb twins he asked no word, he asked her
only of her own self, and of that demon who had
but so recently gone from her. She told in so low
a voice those but a few yards away could not
hear, and Mr. Mather several times cried out,
'Louder — an it please the wench.' She told of
her father and mother in Brittany, and the night
that Mr. Bilby died. She told of the long winter,
and the expectations of the spring and the fulfil-
ment of these expectations — for the messenger
had come, a most vigorous and comely fiend.
Sometimes she reddened and turned away as
might a modest Christian woman. Sometimes
she sighed, and once or twice she smiled a small

and secret smile. And three times she said she
loved and did not fear the demon, and that he
had been kind and pitiful to her.

Judge Bride: You say this devil was your
lover and that he conducted himself as
has many a shameless mortal man to many
a woman, for he loved you, and when he had
stayed himself of you he went away, whis-
tling, we may presume, and shrugging his
shoulders — ah, gentlemen, how shocking
is the conduct of the male, be he demon or
tomcat! And now, Doll Bilby, we are almost to the end. Do not fear to weary us
with the length and detail of your history.
Come, tell us more. The ears of Justice
must ever be long and patient ears.

She told more. There was nothing left untold,
and where she would have turned aside, Judge
Bride encouraged and helped her. Mr. Zelley
moaned and cried out, and his head was in his
hands. Titus went ghostly white and, trembling,
staggered from the room.

Judge Bride: But did not your conscience
hurt? Did you not know that you lived
with this strange lover of yours in sin?

Doll Bilby: I begged him to marry me. So he did.

Judge Bride: A most virtuous and homely
fiend. And did you find clerk or magistrate
to register your vows?

Doll Bilby: No, we married ourselves.

Judge Bride: Ah, the Governor of Connecticut
but recently gave you example.

And he pointed out to Judge Lollimour with
much leisure how evil is bad example in high
places. He questioned Doll further. She told
him all there was to tell about the marriage, and
it humiliated her to tell that she had accepted
this fiend before marriage.

Judge Bride: Come, come, is it then so sorry
a sin for two young people to be too hot
and previous in their love? Surely honest
marriage may be considered salve to such
misconduct.

He glanced through his notes. There was not
a sound in the room, not the scamper of a mouse,
not the taking of breath, no sound except the
fiery rustle of the flares and the crackle of the
paper.

Judge Bride: Doll Bilby, I notice that the
children spoke often of a pretty babe —
which they called yours. Now to what do
they refer?

Doll Bilby: Sir, I cannot be sure.

Judge Bride: You may guess, perhaps?

Doll Bilby: Oh, sir, sir . . .

Her eyes sought Mr. Zelley, but his face was in his hands.

Judge Bride: Speak freely.

Doll Bilby: I think it was to my own babe they referred.

Judge Bride: And where now is this child?

Doll Bilby: It is not yet born.

Judge Bride: And to whom the honour of its paternity?

Doll Bilby: Who else would it be but the fiend who came to comfort me?

Judge Bride: Do not hang your head, young Bilby, for to conceive is natural to woman. Rather should you redden and look down if after such expenditure of infernal ardour you had proved sterile. Conception is the glory of woman.

He stood up and dismissed the hearing. Then Captain Buzzey in a great sweat of fear took the witch back to her cell, and all others went home. That night the Boston Judges lay at the Black Moon. The barmaid heard Judge Lollimour say to Judge Bride, as these two sat by the hearth and drank their sack-posset: 'Sir, this hearing is done as quickly as ever you prophesied. We will be back to Boston on the third day. I warrant the finding is more than any expected. There is enough against the wench to hang her three times over — but that is yet for the magistrates of the Superior Court to decide. We, at least, shall hold her without bail or bond.' Then he said in wonder, 'To think that God has vouchsafed to our eyes the sight of a woman who has embraced a demon . . .' The Judges whispered. The barmaid would not repeat what they said.

These learned men called for ink-horn, sand, and pens. By ten o'clock they had written thus:

Doll Bilby of Cowan Corners, (Essex County,) being this day brought before us upon suspicion of witchcraft and upon the specific charge of afflicting Labour and Sorrow Thumb, twin daughters of Deacon Ephraim Thumb, we heard the aforesaid, and seeing what we did see, together with hearing charges of the persons then present, we committed this same Doll Bilby (she denying the matter of fact, yet confessing herself a witch, also confessing having had carnal knowledge of a fiend, also to being at this time pregnant by him, also to being married to him by the ceremony of Max Pax Fax) unto their majesties' jail at Salem, as per mittimus then given out in order to further examination.

ADAM BRIDE
RALPH LOLLIMOUR } *Magistrates*

By eleven they slept upon their beds.

4

Doll, having cooked her goose, now must sit to eat it. And one who later proves a warlock comes to sit by her side.

Next day Doll rose early, thinking she would be called again before the magistrates. Judge Bride had talked kindly to her and at the end nothing had been said about the Thumb twins. She had not guessed his mind to be made up against her.

She rose early, an hour before dawn, and by a rushlight prepared herself for court. The jailor, John Ackes, could watch her through a chink in the masonry. He saw her put on hat and cloak and set out wooden pattens. He ran in fear to the Black Moon where Mr. Zelley that night lay, and begged him — if he dared — to come a-running, for he believed the witch was about to fly though the roof. She was all dressed and set to go.

Mr. Zelley went to the dungeon and found her waiting to be taken before the magistrates. He sat upon her straw bed by her side, and he took her hands. He said, 'Poor child, lay by your hat and riding-gear, for 'tis all done.'

Done? She had thought they were but started. The matter of the Thumb twins was not yet proven — Judge Bride himself had confessed as much. Mr. Zelley said that now there was another warrant for her and another *mittimus*. But Mr. Zelley must have heard Judge Bride say there was no offence in having seen a devil — had not even Christ talked with Lucifer? And obviously the magistrates had approved her marriage and had even forgiven her that she had been too pliant to her lover's desires. How, therefore, could the Court be done with her — unless they were about to set her free?

'You are to be held for a jury — a jury, my poor Doll, of your own angry neighbours, and for the February sessions of the Superior Court of Judicature.' He explained that Judges Bride and Lollimour could only examine her and hold her over to a higher court. It is true they could have dismissed her as innocent — if it had pleased them; but they could not give sentence of death . . . He wished her to think of death and it might be to prepare her mind and more especially her soul (if she had a soul) against this likely contingence.

'Death?' she said. 'How can I die? God, God, oh, God! I do not want to die.' At the first moment she was afraid of death like any other wicked woman. She closed her eyes and leaned back against the masonry of her cell, remaining a long, long time silent, but her lips moved. Mr. Zelley sat beside her. His head was in his hands. When next she spoke she had conquered fear of death. She spoke bravely in a clear, strong voice. Then she told Mr. Zelley more concerning the fiend whom Hell had sent to love her. She said that he had promised her that, when she should come to die, he would stand at her bed's head. After death he would be with her and she with him forever and ever. She said boldly that she did not fear to die. But she flung herself to her knees and laid her tousled head in Mr. Zelley's lap and then confessed that she had a most hideous horror of gallows and halter. As he could he comforted her. Tears streamed from his eyes, though hers were always dry. He knelt and seemed to pray to God.

John Ackes at his chink saw him pray and heard his prayer. He said it was an unseemly prayer — not like those one hears in church — not like the majestic and awful utterances of Mr. Increase Mather. Zelley talked to God as you might talk to a friend. So many thought that it was not to the true God that he prayed, but to some demon whom he privately worshipped. When his own day came to hang, this thing was remembered against him.

The witch-woman crouched upon her straw bed the while he prayed. She had put her hat on her head again and was wrapped in her scarlet riding-coat. She stared out of round cat's eyes at the man who prayed for her.

5

Abortive attempts to save a SOUL and more infernal manifestations of the Demon Lover.

Now was her physical body in sore plight, for she was bound in irons heavier than a strong man might bear. The jailors feared her, and, although an eye was forever at the chink, they did as little for her as might be. The Court permitted only these to go to her: her jailors; the two ministers of God, labouring in Salem, and Mr. Increase Mather whose mind was at that time big with a demonology. He wished to study and examine her. It was three weeks before Mr. Zelley got a permit from Boston to visit her. He guessed by the cold, tardy manner in which his request was answered that he himself had fallen into ill-repute. This was true. His people thought him a warlock and feared and hated him.

When twenty years later, in the days of the great witch-hunting and hanging in Salem, Mr. Zelley himself came to be tried, John Ackes was commanded to tell the Court (if he could remember) of what it was the witch and the warlock had talked through those long hours they had sat side by side upon the witch's straw bed. He testified (swearing to his truth upon the Bible) that they talked but little. Zelley's head was forever in his hands. He did not see the witch-woman's face — nor her eyes. He did not see how constantly she gaped at empty corners; how she smiled and nodded into space; how sometimes she would close her eyes and raise her mouth for the empty air to kiss. All this she did behind Mr. Zelley's back. They asked John Ackes if Mr. Zelley made no attempt to save the woman's soul. No, he only sat. Sometimes he talked a little to Doll and sometimes he talked to one whom he designated as 'god.' But he did not really pray at all — not as Mr. Mather prayed — him you could hear through stone walls and up and down the street. The crowd would gather outside the jail when Mr. Mather prayed. He was a most fearful and righteous suppliant before the Throne of God. After his prayers the wonder was no lightning came to destroy the young witch where she sat — grimacing and leering at spectres. When one considered Mr. Mather, one could not say that Zelley prayed at all.

However, it was true that Zelley would sometimes seem to beg Doll Bilby to turn to God before it was too late. She would always explain to him that she wanted no other God than Lucifer and no Heaven, for where her parents were and her foster father and her dear husband — there with them was her Paradise, not in Heaven with the cold angels singing psalms forever to an angry and awful God; not in Heaven where

199

doubtless Hannah Bilby would be found and all her cruel neighbours — no, no, a thousand times no. Hell was her true home — her Paradise.

Sometimes he would read to her from a stout big book, and John Ackes swore he thought it was a Bible, although it was possible that the book was a book of magic — perhaps this was even probable. Still the stories he read to her from this book sounded to him like Bible stories. What would he read to her? He read to her of Mary of Magdala, how she laid her head upon our Saviour's feet and wiped them with her hair. He read to her the holy promises of John. It was evident, said John Ackes, that Zelley was not for a long time conscious of the fiend which lurked forever in the witch's cell.

Towards the end no one but Mr. Zelley dared go to her dungeon. They were all afraid. It was remembered and marked against him that, where other and more godly men felt fear, he felt no fear. At last even Mr. Zelley knew that he and the witch were never alone. There was another and more awful presence about.

Now he would look up quickly from his reading and catch her eyes as they sought those of some one or something close behind his own shoulder. When their eyes met, she would smile so softly and happily he knew that the invisible presence must be that of the one she loved. Mr. Zelley confessed that this consciousness of a third and unseen party in the cell sadly upset and confused him. He sweated, he could not read. One afternoon she gave him such close attention he decided that the fiend had left, so he closed his book and asked her abruptly if her demon lover had come back again. She was surprised that he asked this question. 'Of course he is back,' she said. 'Now he will not leave me until the end.' It was not he, she said, whom the Thumb twins saw at the trial, and Doll again wickedly said that perhaps that creature had been an angel. 'My fiend never came near me as I stood all day on trial. Now he has sworn to stay with me. If I go to Gallows Hill, he will go with me. If I die here first, he will hold my hands.'

Zelley asked her if she could really see this demon. For instance, was he at that very moment in the room? Oh, yes. He sat yonder by the cupboard. His head, she said, rested upon his bosom. 'Last night I had a fearful fit of terror. I thought I could not face the gallows.

He held me in his arms and sang to me until sunrise. Now he sleeps.'

'Is he now in seaman's clothes and has he the likeness of proper man?' (Mr. Zelley whispered. He feared to wake the demon.)

'No. He has returned in shape of true fiend. For he is horned, naked, scaly, black. His feet are cloven. He has vast leathery bat-pinions. His tail is long and spiked.'

'How, then, can you know that this is your own fiend and not another one?'

'By his eyes and by his loving voice. These things have not changed.'

'How is it he returned to you? In what manner did he make himself manifest?'

'You recall that day after the trial when you came to me and let me know beyond a doubt that I must die? All the next day I felt him in the cell with me. Then little by little he took visible form. At first he was a vapour that seemed to rise between the flags of the dungeon floor, and then I could see the shadow of his great and most awful form — a transparent shadow through which one could look, even as one looks through smoke. But daily he gained more and more in body and he now is as hard

202

and sturdy as mortal man. At first seeing horns, tail, and so fearsome a scaly black body, I cried out in my disappointment and despair. I, in my simplicity, had imagined he would always be to me as he had been — shaped, dressed, and coloured like comely, mortal man. He seemed monstrous to me — more likely to inspire fear than love. At last I could see his eyes and they were unchanged. And his voice (for, having gained complete actuality, he could speak) was the same. So I knew him as my own husband, and now I love him more in his present infernal majesty than I did in seaman's form. This shape is fairer to me.' (Thus twenty years later Mr. Zelley testified in court as to his conversation with Doll Bilby.)

On being pressed, Mr. Zelley confessed still further. He said he asked her why it was that no one — not even the jailors — dared go to her cell. Did they fear the spectral presence? She was amazed that he had heard no gossip. Surely the village must by now be buzzing with the tricks her demon had performed. Had he not heard what had befallen her peeping jailors? They used (to her unutterable torment and vexation) watch her through a chink in the masonry.

But the demon punished them by blowing into
their eyes. This had given them the pink-eye.
Surely he must have noticed that her jailors suffered from pink-eye? Now that she mentioned it
he said he believed he had noticed it. And she
was to tell him further. Why did the great Mr.
Mather come no more? She clapped her hands,
laughing and purring. Her demon had hated Mr.
Mather so bitterly, and had so resented his long,
loud prayers, that he had several times been on
the point of strangling him. In his utter foolish-
ness the man had dared to read the story of
Tobit to her — how Sara was beloved of the
fiend Asmodeus and how this fiend strangled her
many husbands upon their marriage beds, but
how at the last this fine fiend Asmodeus had
been driven to farthest Egypt by the stench of
a burning fish's liver. This story the wicked
witch claimed to be utterly false — it made no
jot of difference to her that it was found in Holy
Writ. She said it was a black lie that did much
to minimize that dignity of Prince Asmodeus —
who was a close friend to her own lover. She
put up her hand and whispered to Mr. Zelley
that, although her fiend had never told her his
own true name, she had reason to suspect that

he himself was none other than this same Asmodeus, for he was touchy beyond all reason for
the dignity of the Prince and he had told her at
some length how dull, tedious, and complaining
a woman Sara had been, and how gladly her
lover had surrendered her in the end to the young
Jew. The burning fish's liver had never driven
him forth — he went as it pleased himself. The
stench had almost expelled the bride from her
bridal chamber, but it had had no effect upon
the stalwart demon Prince.

Mr. Mather had insisted on reading this story
thrice over to her, and on the last reading he had
also endeavoured to burn the large liver of a cod-
fish. Then her husband rushed at the fire. His
tail stood up rigid in rage; he shook his horns
like an angry bull; he rustled his vast pinions,
and, as he snuffed out the fire that made the
stench with his two horny hands, Mr. Mather
looked up and of a sudden saw him there and
was close to dying of terror. Doll begged the
fiend again to assume invisibility and not to
strangle the distinguished Divine. So Mr.
Mather went away and never came again. But
surely, surely Mr. Zelley had heard this thing
spoken of? And how her demon had served the

two Salem clergymen — the tricks he had put on them — surely these things were common gossip? No, of these things he had heard never a word. No one gossiped with him — now.

It was then at that moment he first came to know he was under suspicion. Doll knew this too. She told him how she had never heard that the Thumb twins were bewitched until the very day Captain Buzzey rode up and accused her of their bewitchment. She said she pitied Mr. Zelley and he said his life grew strange. Every one in all the world was far removed, and even God had turned His face away from him. He said (foolishly) that all his life he had felt that if he believed in witches, demons, etc., he could not believe in God; for that God Whom he worshipped would not tolerate such evil things. Yet now had he seen the proof that such things were true — and, if true, where, then, was that great and good God whom he had long worshipped? 'My Doll,' he said, 'you have taken away my reason and my God — now I have nothing. I have not even one man I may call "friend."'

She comforted him, not by words, but by putting her small hands (now thin as a bird's claws) upon his bent head. She kissed his forehead. He got up and went away. He did not stay as he should have stayed with his flock in Cowan Corners. He slept at the Black Moon, for such was the bewitchment that Doll had set upon him he must see her again and that early upon the next day.

6

The Labours of a Witch and the Prayers of the Godly.

The year was nine days old and no more. Then was Doll Bilby taken in labour and brought prematurely to bed.

The Salem midwife — ancient Nan Hackett — would have none of her, and it seemed that, whatever it was she must bear, she should bear alone. Nor did she ask for mortal aid. She was content with that phantom which stood night and day (as many saw) at her bed's head. Mr. Zelley remembered that Goody Goochey, when first she came to Cowan Corners, had served the beginning as well as the end of life — that is, she had been a midwife as well as a layer-out of the dead. He went to the woman and begged her, in pity's name and partly commanded her in the name of the General Court, to get herself to Salem jail and there give such service as might be.

She was afraid. She did not wish to be mid-wife to a witch and the first to welcome a black imp into the world. She drank three piggins of ale and took a leather bottle of brandy with her. She set upon her thumbs and fingers those iron rings with which she was accustomed to guard herself against the ghosts of the dead. She thought, after all, is not a live imp of greater danger to a good Christian's soul than the body of a dead church elder? Mr. Zelley went with her to the jail.

The witch at the moment was not in pain. She lay with eyes black as the pits of Hell. Her white mouth was open. She roused herself a little and made Mr. Zelley a brief speech in which she said that she had, as he knew, sought God and spiritual peace, and now, let him look into her face and say that she had failed to find either. It was true, said Mr. Zelley. Her face was fulfilled of heavenly peace. He left her without a word.

Outside he found a conclave of idle men and women who laughed and joked coarsely. One big ruddy wench (who had already borne, to the embarrassment of the community, three fatherless children) was crying out loudly that

God knew it was enough for woman to give birth
to human child, which is round and sleek as a
melon. God help the witch now in labour with
an imp, for it would come into the world with
spiked tail and horns. Such a thing would be the
death of any mortal woman. All were afraid.
Some believed a clap of thunder would come
down from Heaven and destroy the woman.
Others that a fiend would rise up from Hell to
succour her. Some said that the witches and
warlocks for an hundred miles had gathered
together and now, mounting broomsticks, were
about to charge down upon Salem. One said,
'Have you not heard? Judge Bride has suffered
an apoplexy. Judge Lollimour is at death's
door.' This was not so.

Another said Captain Tom Buzzey's hands
(those hands that had held the witch) had
withered. They had shrivelled to the size of
a child's. This was not so.

All said the witch is in labour. She's with
child by the Devil. God will burn her soul in
Hell. This was so.

The day wore on. The sun, as sometimes
may be in the midst of winter, was so warm the
snow melted and water dripped from the eaves

of the jail. It was tender as a day in spring. Planks and rugs were laid in the slush, for certain clergymen came to pray and must have dry land to kneel upon. They prayed that God recollect the number of good, pious Christian people there were at Salem and not destroy all, for they feared His wrath might blast the whole village. God made no sign, but the water dripped from the eaves and a sweet spring fragrance rose from the melting snow.

The multitude gaped and feared. Sometimes they smelt sulphur, saltpeter, brimstone, and the stench as of a sloughing serpent. They heard the crying of a phantom voice and the swishing of a thousand brooms. So they waited through the day expecting every moment to see crabbed Goody Goochey hobble out with a black imp upon a blanket to show them.

There was no sound from the cell. Not one cry nor moan from the witch, not one word from Goochey. The jailors would open the door. It stuck. Their keys would not fit it. They could not open the door, and believed devils were holding it fast. They dared not peek in the chink because of their pink-eye.

By sundown most went home.

7

Mr. Zelley opens a Dungeon Door, and what came of it.

The next day dawned cold and grey over an icy sea, and the gulls and terns came in from the harbour crying and lamenting. There was now no tenderness in the air, and the water that had but yesterday melted under the rays of a genial sun froze to glassy ice. A wind sharp as needles came in off the sea and few if any watched the night out on their knees beside the dungeon walls. As soon as it was possible to see six feet ahead, the multitude again began to assemble, but this time they came without laughter or conversation. They were shrouded in hoods, shawls, etc., for warmth, and seemed a spectral band. Now and then one or another of them would raise a pious voice in prayer, lamentation, or thanksgiving, but for the most part they stood bowed and mute. All night there had been no sound from the witch's cell — never a sound. Who was there so bold as to enter in to her and bring back a report, for John Ackes's hand shook so he could not manage the key? Some said Mr. Zelley would go — he had no normal, wholesome fear of witches or demons. Others said, 'Where does he lie to-night?' Others, 'Go, run and fetch him'; and a boy (it was Widow Hannah's bonded boy Jake Tulley) said the man lay at the Black Moon and that he would run and fetch him. This he did.

Mr. Zelley came in a steeple hat and a greatcoat. He spoke to no one. No one spoke to him. He entered the jail and took the cell key from Ackes, and, after some shaking and effort, he turned the lock and pushed hard on the door, which swung in so suddenly he almost fell on his knees beside that straw bed where he had sat so many wicked hours with the witch-girl. A hundred had crowded down the passage and into the doorway after Mr. Zelley. All stopped at the threshold of the cell. They stood agape, some filled with curiosity, some with fear, others with pious ejaculations and elevated thoughts.

Goody Goochey (who indeed proved to be no woman, but a man) lay in a drunken fit in a corner. His face was purple and his throat twisted and bruised as though he had been half strangled — which he always averred to his dying day was the truth, for he had seen the scaly black demon come at him with great hands outstretched to his throat, and that was the last he could really remember until certain ones tumbled him out into the snow. He was sure, however, that, as he lay thus almost unconscious in a corner, a great concourse of spectrals and infernals had filled the cell. They had danced, sung, and made much of the witch, praising her, encouraging her, etc. Because the man was known to be an impostor (he had for many years made all think him a woman) and because of his swinish, drunken ways, many did not believe what he said.

All could see that Bilby's Doll was dead. She lay with her round eyes open to the ceiling, and her expression was one of peace and content. Whatever she might have borne was dead within her.

8

Without HELL *where is* HEAVEN? *And without a Devil where is* GOD? *Also the last of Doll Bilby and an end to these instructions.*

There are court records, affidavits, etc.; there are diaries, letters and such; there is the memory of old gaffers and goodies to prove that once Doll Bilby flourished. But of physical, inanimate objects nothing that was associated with her evil life and awful end now exists. The house she lived in mysteriously rotted and fell into the cellar hole. The grave they dug her is now lost under a ploughed field (a sterile field that yields little). Where the dungeon was now is a brick house, a fine big house of red bricks had out from England. No one will live there. Yet any gamin, for a copper penny, and any courting couple, for wanton pleasure, will show you the very spot in the white birch thicket where Doll met her demon lover night after night under the moonlight, in that world of witchery which none to-day will ever see. For in those days there were sights and wonders that will not come again. In those days God was nearer to man than He is to-day, and where God is there also must be His Evil Opponent — the Prince of Lies, for show me Paradise, and there, around a corner, I will show you Hell.

Finis coronat opus